Also by E. D. Baker

More Than a PRINCESS

E. D. BAKER

BLOOMSBURY
CHILDREN'S BOOKS
NEW YORK LONDON OXFORD NEW DELHI SYDNEY

BLOOMSBURY CHILDREN'S BOOKS
Bloomsbury Publishing Inc., part of Bloomsbury Publishing Plc
1385 Broadway, New York, NY 10018

BLOOMSBURY, BLOOMSBURY CHILDREN'S BOOKS, and the Diana logo
are trademarks of Bloomsbury Publishing Plc

First published in the United States of America in November 2018
by Bloomsbury Children's Books

Bloomsbury books may be purchased for business or promotional use. For information
on bulk purchases please contact Macmillan Corporate and Premium Sales Department at
specialmarkets@macmillan.com

Library of Congress Cataloging-in-Publication Data
Names: Baker, E. D., author.
Title: More than a princess / by E. D. Baker.
Description: New York : Bloomsbury, 2018.
Summary: Aislin of Eliasind must rely on more than the magical gifts she has as a
half-fairy, half-pedrasi when she becomes entangled in a sinister plot and
saddled with difficult human princesses.
Identifiers: LCCN 2018003772 (print) | LCCN 2018010441 (e-book)
ISBN 978-1-68119-768-5 (hardcover) • ISBN 978-1-68119-771-5 (e-book)
Subjects: | CYAC: Fairy tales. | Princesses—Fiction. | Magic—Fiction. | Fairies—Fiction. |
Self-confidence—Fiction.
Classification: LCC PZ8.B173 Mor 2018 (print) | LCC PZ8.B173 (e-book) | DDC [Fic]—dc23
LC record available at https://lccn.loc.gov/2018003772

Book design by Danielle Ceccolini
Typeset by Westchester Publishing Services
Printed and bound in the U.S.A. by Berryville Graphics Inc., Berryville, Virginia
2 4 6 8 10 9 7 5 3 1

To find out more about our authors and books visit www.bloomsbury.com and sign up for
our newsletters.

THIS BOOK IS DEDICATED TO KIM, ELLIE, KEVIN,
SOPHIE, VICTORIA, AND ALL MY FANS, WHOSE
ENTHUSIASM KEEPS ME WRITING.

Chapter 1

"Now open your eyes," King Carrigan commanded.

Aislin gasped when she saw the glamour that her father had created. Nearly all her senses told her that she and all the other children who lived in the castle were perched on small, puffy clouds high in the sky, looking down at the mountains below.

"Look at that!" her little brother, Timzy, said, pointing at something on the ground.

Aislin glanced over the side of her cloud and saw that he was pointing at their very own castle nestled in the forest, its white walls glowing in the last sunlight of the day. She turned to Timzy and smiled when he gushed, "That's our home! I've never seen it from this high before. Thank you, Papa. This is wonderful!"

It was Timzy's seventh birthday, and their father had created an extra-special glamour for the party. King Carrigan of Eliasind was such a powerful fairy that the glamour was thoroughly convincing, even down to the cold damp of the clouds beneath them and the warmth of the sun on their backs.

"This is so beautiful!" said Poppy, a red-haired fairy, from the cloud beside Aislin's. "I've never been this high up before. My wings aren't strong enough to carry me this far."

Poppy was the same age as Aislin; she had lived in the castle all her life and had been Aislin's closest friend since the days when they played together as toddlers. Poppy had come into her fairy abilities just a few months before, and though Aislin was happy for her friend, she couldn't help but feel a pang of jealousy every time she saw Poppy get small and sprout wings.

Aislin was half fairy, but she couldn't do many of the things that fairies could do. Though she was proud of both sides of her heritage, sometimes it really bothered her that she was more pedrasi than fairy; her strongest connection was to the ground, not the sky. More than anything, she wished that she could fly! Pedrasi often joked that they had stone dust in their veins. Aislin wondered if it was true, and if it was actually weighing her down, preventing her from doing all the things she wanted to do.

A flock of birds flew below them, unaware of its audience. The sun was setting to the east, the darkness sweeping toward the mountains. Some of the children laughed and clapped their hands as a griffin flew past, looking surprised to see people so high in the sky. When Aislin turned to the north, where the land between the mountains stretched into the distance, she could see past her parents' kingdom, Eliasind, to the mountain called Deephold where her pedrasi grandparents lived. A flash of light caught her eye as the sun's rays reflected off Fairengar, the fairies' crystal palace, far off at the northernmost point. Although Aislin knew this was all an illusion, it seemed so real!

As the clouds drifted above the landscape, something else caught Aislin's eye.

She turned to her father. The golden-haired king appeared to be standing on a cloud with Aislin's mother, enjoying the looks of wonder on the children's faces. "What is that just past the mountains?" Aislin asked, pointing at the green hills that lay to the south of the mountain range.

"That's Scarmander," her father replied. "And that's Morain," he added, pointing to the east.

 3

"Are those human kingdoms, Your Highness?" asked Bim, the tiny sprite boy.

"They are," said the king. "Even before the fairies left the human world, those two kingdoms were always declaring war on each other." The children shuddered.

"What if the humans see us up here?" asked a little fairy girl seated next to Aislin.

"They can't...," Aislin began, but Timzy was already getting to his feet.

"Don't worry, I'll protect you!" the little boy cried. "I'm not afraid of any silly old humans."

As children stood, following the example of their young prince, King Carrigan laughed. "Enough of that!" he said. "I hear we have some other entertainment waiting for you."

Suddenly the glamour of the clouds dissolved and the children found themselves back in the Great Hall, with their parents' smiling faces all around them. At a signal from the king, four pedrasi men strode into the center of the hall and began to juggle brightly colored stones. Even without seeing them up close, Aislin could sense that the stones were rubies, emeralds, and citrines.

Aislin knew all four men; like many of the adults there, they worked in the castle. Some had come with

Maylin, Aislin's mother and pedrasi princess, when she had married the fairy prince. More pedrasi arrived after Maylin and Carrigan were made king and queen of their own kingdom, Eliasind. Still others had joined the household over the years as word spread of the welcome all fey received at the mixed court.

Aislin and the other children laughed when a tiny fairy riding a wren intercepted a stone and carried it off. The pedrasi men continued to juggle, pretending to be upset as their stones disappeared, "stolen" by one small fairy after another. When the jugglers were down to one stone apiece, they gave up and took their bows to loud applause.

A pair of full-sized fairies took their place, calling for volunteers. After choosing a pedrasi boy, a fairy girl, and an ogre brother and sister, they turned the children into frogs, delighting the others as they hopped around. The children sat entranced as the fairies caught the frogs and turned them into butterflies, then doves, and finally back into children again. The rest of the enraptured audience demanded their turns, each shouting out which animal they would like to be. Aislin laughed when all the sprites wanted to be dragons.

She sat back, content to watch the younger children enjoy themselves. As she looked around the hall, just seeing the looks of delight on all the different faces made her happy. Green-skinned nymphs with vines twined in their hair clapped and shouted encouragement. Coarse-featured ogres, who each stood over eight feet tall, roared with laughter when an ogre boy became a bumblebee and buzzed past. Seven-inch-tall sprites swung from the banners hanging from the ceiling, calling out suggestions to the fairies. Their tiny children were dragons for less than a minute; their turns ended when they started breathing fire.

Aislin noticed that both the pedrasi and the fairies were beaming at the joy on their children's faces. It was easy to tell one group from the other. The pedrasi, the people of the mountains, were shorter and sturdier than the fairykind. Few stood over four and a half feet tall. Their dense bones and powerful muscles made them strong enough to lift heavy rocks, and their large pupils allowed them to see in the almost-absolute dark of the caverns that were their ancestral homes. All full-blooded pedrasi had dark hair, and their fair skin bronzed readily when they left the depths of their caverns to live in the sunlight of the land between the mountains.

Although the pedrasi were generally a handsome people, they weren't nearly as attractive as the ethereal fairies. Aislin's father's kin stood taller than six feet when full-sized, and had the ability to shrink small enough to ride a wren. When fairies made themselves tiny, they sprouted butterfly-like wings from between their shoulder blades, enabling them to fly. Their wings were only strong enough to carry them short distances, to be true, but still they reveled in the magic, flitting about through the castle and forest. When they were full-sized, the fairies' narrow bones made them fragile looking, but this was deceptive, because they were actually quite strong. To some, fairies' long, thin fingers, narrow faces, distinctly colored eyes, and pointed ears made them look striking, though Aislin considered them as normal as the sturdier pedrasi. All fairies were beautiful; Queen Surinen, the queen of the fairies and Aislin's grandmother, was said to be the most beautiful of all.

Aislin was flattered when told that she looked like her grandmother, though she knew it wasn't exactly true. While they both had dark hair and violet eyes, the fairy queen's features were more delicate and refined. Aislin's face wasn't nearly as narrow and her ears didn't have pointed tips. Her pedrasi side made her body sturdier and her figure nicely rounded (all the better to fend off the chill of the mountains,

Aislin thought). She also had the large pedrasi pupils that many found so attractive, but that made bright light almost painful to absorb. One thing that she certainly had in common with her grandmother was that they were both even more beautiful when they smiled.

Aside from such marked similarities to her grandmother, Aislin was unique.

As Aislin turned her attention back to the festivities, the last child had been given a turn to try a different animal form and the pedrasi cook was stepping forward. Calling out in a ringing voice, Cook announced, "I hope you're ready for supper, children, because the feast is ready for you!"

The little ones cheered, though the voices of the adult sprites were even louder as everyone hurried to move the tables and benches back to their normal places. When the room was ready and each guest had taken his or her seat, the servers appeared, carrying in course after course. The food was as delightfully varied as the attendees. There were berries and greens for the nymphs, crunchy grain for the lone satyr, hearty stews and root vegetables for the pedrasi, honeyed blossoms and fresh fruit for the fairies, and broiled sturgeon for the ogres. The creamy custards, flaky pastries, and berry-filled pies were supposed to be for everyone, but the sprites ate most of the desserts.

The sprites who finished early scurried up the tapestries decorating the walls, scampering along the exposed beams of the ceilings and shimmying down the banners that fluttered above the tables. Some of the more mischievous among them started to throw their weight back and forth, making the banners sway. No one minded much—that is, until they launched themselves onto the tables, doing flips and somersaults on their way down, and landing on half-filled platters, in people's laps, and into freshly refilled tankards. When one fell into the bowl of stew in front of an ogre, splashing him full in the face, the ogre's roar was enough to shake the hall. The sprites didn't stop playing, though, until the servers brought out the birthday cakes, ablaze with candles.

Spotting the cakes, the sprites descended on the servers. The cook was ready for them, however, and she shooed them away. "I know you lot snuck into the kitchen and licked the icing off the little cakes!" she said. "So those are all yours. I already put more icing on them and they're waiting for you at your table. Now off with you, and no more of this foolishness!"

The sprites continued to eye the bigger cakes even

as they returned to their table, but their grumbling stopped when they spotted the tiny cakes waiting for them. They started gobbling their cakes as if they hadn't eaten in weeks.

The rest of the cake was eaten nearly as quickly, with birthday boy Timzy getting a piece as big as the ogres' share. Timzy and Aislin were still eating their slices when their pedrasi tutor, Nurlue, stood up. At five foot two, he was taller than most pedrasi, and he had an impressively full salt-and-pepper beard that covered much of his chest.

"Since I have you all together," Nurlue said, glancing from one child to the next, "I believe that this is a good time for a lesson."

While the children groaned, their parents grinned. Aislin set down her fork and leaned forward to watch Nurlue.

"Because we have a new family in our midst, we have planned a small demonstration of pedrasi abilities," he said, bowing to the ogre family who had only recently moved in. "I understand that you moved here from a cave near Fairengar. Few pedrasi live in that area, so you may not know much about us. If I tell you that we have 'rock magic,' you still may not know what I mean, so we're going to give you an idea of what we can do. Your Majesty, if you would care to go first?"

The queen smiled as she left the dais and strode to the middle of the hall. "I'd like all the children to join me here," she said, and waited while they gathered around her. When the children were seated, she continued. "Those who aren't familiar with our court might think that I, as queen, do nothing more than sit on a throne giving orders or retire to my chamber to embroider, but that is not the case. Everyone in Eliasind helps out, including me. Does anyone have any aches or pains today?"

The children turned to look at each other to see who would answer. Finally, Poppy spoke up, saying, "I burned my hand helping in the kitchen yesterday."

Because Poppy was still a child, she didn't have a job, but she did help out wherever she could. It was an excellent way to figure out what she liked doing so she could pick the job she wanted when it was time.

Queen Maylin gestured to the fairy girl, who made her way between the other children until she reached the queen. When Poppy stuck out her hand, Aislin could see the bright-red mark on her palm. Queen Maylin held her own hand over it so they were almost, but not quite, touching. The queen closed her eyes, and everyone held their breath in anticipation. Aislin glanced at the stone floor. She could feel a trickle of power flowing into her mother, drawn from the stone itself. When she looked up, a warm pink light had enveloped the two hands.

The light faded away and the queen smiled at Poppy. "Is that better?" Queen Maylin asked the fairy girl.

Poppy flexed her hand and nodded. "Much better," she replied. "The burn is gone, like it was never there! Thank you so much."

"Is there anyone else who needs my help?" the queen asked as Poppy returned to stand beside Aislin.

"My wrist hurts," said an ogre boy.

"I have a tummy ache," groaned Bim.

"That's because you ate so many cakes!" his father called from the banner overhead.

Everyone who knew Bim laughed, aware of his insatiable appetite for sweets.

A line formed as a few other children proclaimed their aches and pains. It didn't take long for the queen to heal them as well. The party guests applauded as Queen Maylin returned to the dais.

Once again Nurlue stepped forward. "Fluric, Dinsel, if you wouldn't mind demonstrating?"

Two young pedrasi men walked to the middle of the hall carrying buckets filled with rocks. While Fluric poured the rocks out onto the floor, Dinsel put on a blindfold. Fluric checked Dinsel's blindfold to make sure he really couldn't see, then turned to the crowd in the hall. "I need a volunteer," he said, choosing Timzy when the young prince's hand shot up.

Timzy hurried to the man's side and looked up at him expectantly.

"Please pick up a rock and place it in Dinsel's hands, Your Grace," said Fluric.

Timzy took his time picking up a rock.

"Granite," the blindfolded man announced.

Fluric took a closer look at the rock. "It is," he announced.

Timzy handed Dinsel another rock.

"Quartz," Dinsel declared.

"That's right," Fluric said after looking at it.

They went through a dozen rocks that way, with Timzy picking them up randomly and Dinsel getting each one right. After Dinsel declared that another rock was also granite, he took off his blindfold and bowed to Timzy. "Thank you for your help, Your Grace."

Timzy grinned and turned to sit down, but Dinsel stopped him. "Just a moment, Your Grace. Please stay right there." Holding the rock high, Dinsel turned so that everyone could see it. "Granite is very special to me. When I need it, I can draw great strength from granite." Dinsel, still holding the rock, walked up to an ogre seated on a chair and picked up the chair, ogre and all. Everyone in the hall clapped.

"Nearly everyone who is at least part pedrasi has a kind of rock that is special to them. We have determined that Prince Timzy's is lapis lazuli. Your Grace, we would like to present this amulet to you. Your pedrasi side will let you tap into the stone when the need arises. Nurlue will teach you how to use it as part of your lessons."

"Thank you!" Timzy said, his face lighting up as he took the blue amulet dangling from a heavy gold chain. Aislin guessed that he could already feel at least some connection with the stone.

He was on his way to sit with the other children when the fairy woman Larch approached him. Larch was tall and thin, with pure white hair and skin that might have belonged to a very young woman, although everyone knew that she'd once been Queen Maylin's nursemaid and was incredibly old. Like all fairies, she was beautiful, but she had kinder eyes than most and always seemed to know what children were thinking.

She had been Aislin and Timzy's nursemaid when they were little, too, and still spent her time looking out for them.

"We fairies would like to give you something as well," Larch told him. "May I see your amulet?"

At first Timzy looked as if he didn't want to give it up, but when she reached for it, he reluctantly held it out to her. Cradling it in one hand, she whispered a few words, then passed her other hand over it. Fairy dust sparkled around the stone for a few moments, then seemed to settle on it before melting away.

"I've placed a protection spell on your amulet," Larch told the prince. "It will alert you when danger is near and help you defend yourself."

Timzy looked excited when he took the amulet back from her. "Thanks!" he said, and hurried to his seat on the floor.

He slipped the chain over his head. Aislin crouched down beside him. "May I see it?" she asked, her hand hovering inches from the stone.

"Sure, but I'm not taking it off," her brother told her.

"You don't have to," she said, sensing the magic in it before she'd even touched it with her fingertips.

"Isn't it great?" he cried. "Now I can be superstrong, too!"

"Uh-huh," she said. She knew the moment she touched it that this was in fact the right stone for Timzy. He was already in tune with it, and it would make him stronger (although not nearly as strong as her or their mother).

"This was an excellent choice for you," Aislin said, removing her hand from the amulet. "Take good care of it."

She was about to walk away when one of the newly arrived ogre children called out, "What is your special rock, Your Grace?"

"I don't have one," she told her.

"Then what is that stone you're wearing?"

Aislin glanced down at the cheery yellow stone dangling from the golden chain she never took off, and blushed. People didn't usually ask about her stone, in part because most already knew what it was and why she wore it. "It's a mood stone," she said. "It was created especially for me. The stone changes color to match my moods."

"What does yellow mean?" the child asked.

"It means I'm happy," Aislin said, and smiled at her.

"Why don't you have a stone to make you stronger?" the little girl persisted.

"Because I don't need it," Aislin replied.

When the girl looked confused, Aislin walked over to the bench where four ogres were sitting with Jasper, the satyr. Planting her feet squarely on the floor, she tapped into the stone she was standing on, pulling its strength into her. The sensation was invigorating; she felt as if she was as connected to the stone as she was to her own body. Although the power that filled her was but a trickle at first, it quickly turned into a stream, making her cheeks flush and the strength of the stone course through her. Bending her knees, she picked up the bench and the people sitting on it. She wasn't even breathing hard. Turning back to the child, she said, "I can draw from any stone."

A roar of approval shook the room as Aislin set the bench down. Jasper and the ogres she had lifted still looked surprised when she walked away.

She had noticed that one of the rocks had tumbled under a nearby table when Fluric dumped them onto the floor. Pointing at the hidden rock, she said, "Return to the bag," in a voice that had a strange quiver to it.

The rock shook and began to roll across the floor. The children cheered when it disappeared inside the bag.

"Our princess has many pedrasi skills, but we think it is her fairy side that makes her skills so strong," said Nurlue as the noise died down.

"What else can you do?" asked the ogre girl's brother.

Aislin shrugged. "The normal pedrasi things, like locate veins of rocks and minerals in the mountains, find fissures, and mend cracks." Aware that too many questions were bound to ruin her good mood, she turned to where Nurlue was sitting. "Isn't it time for some music?"

"Indeed!" Nurlue said, getting to his feet.

A fairy knight holding a lute stood up, along with half a dozen pedrasi men. The knight played a few chords, and the men began to sing. Their voices were deeper than most, their singing enough to make toes tap and people sway in their seats.

The audience seemed to enjoy the music, though after two songs they began to get restless.

"Princess Aislin, please sing for us!" called out a nymph. Other fey picked up the call and soon even the pedrasi men who had been singing joined in.

With a nudge from Poppy, Aislin stepped to the center of the room. She waited until the Great Hall was silent. Like her pedrasi relatives, she loved to sing, but with the added element of fairy, her voice was special and unique. A blend of the nuance-rich tone of a pedrasi and the incredible range of a fairy, Aislin's voice was glorious. She sang a happy song about the tricks flower fairies play on each other, and soon most of her audience was laughing, even though they had all heard it many times before. The only ones who weren't laughing were the ogres, who had fallen into a blank-eyed, mouth-hanging-open stupor as soon as she began to sing, just like they always did. Aislin wasn't sure if that was a good thing or not.

She had just finished her third song when an eagle flew through an open window high on the far wall, carrying a fairy messenger. The moment his feet touched the floor, the messenger became full-sized. All eyes followed him as he strode to the dais where King Carrigan sat beside his queen.

Aislin didn't hear what the messenger said, but she could tell from her father's expression that it wasn't good. Her heart sank when the king gestured to his warriors, who all stood and left the hall behind him.

As Aislin watched them go, Timzy came running over. "Is the party over?"

"I'm afraid so," she replied. "I just wish I knew why."

Chapter 2

THE MOOD STONE DANGLING from the gold chain around Aislin's neck glowed blue-gray against her sun-bronzed skin, but no one needed to look at it to know that the princess was worried. Only an hour before, the messenger had arrived with a summons from her grandparents, the king and queen of the fairies. King Carrigan and his warriors were about to leave for Fair-engar, but Aislin still didn't know why. She'd returned to her room to fetch her good luck charm so her father could take it with him, but so far her search had been fruitless.

"Where is it?" Aislin cried, riffling through the clothes in the trunk by her door. The mirror on the stone mantel rattled as her agitation grew.

"What are you looking for, Princess?" asked a voice from the shadows. A doll, about ten inches tall, slipped off a small chair and pattered across the floor to tug at Aislin's hem. "Is there anything I can do?"

"A messenger told Father his parents have summoned him and that he must leave right away," Aislin told her. "He's never received an urgent summons before, and I'm afraid something bad might be happening. I want to give Father my good luck charm to take with him, but he's leaving in a few minutes and I can't find it."

"I'm sure he'll be all right," the doll said, gazing up at the princess with amethyst eyes. A gift from the fairy queen, Twinket had quickly become one of Aislin's closest friends and was always there for her.

"I wish *I* could be sure!" Aislin cried. A tremor ran through the stone floor.

"Your father is a very powerful fairy," said the doll. "He can handle anything."

"So are my grandparents," said Aislin. "Which means there must be something terribly wrong if they need my father's help."

Twinket was startled when the floor began to shake in earnest, and she had to grab hold of a chair leg so that she wouldn't fall down.

There was one fairy quality that Aislin wished she *didn't* have—her temper. When combined with her pedrasi strength, her emotional reactions could be dangerous to others. This was the reason her two grandmothers had worked together to create the mood stone. When Aislin was an infant, the stone had helped her parents know why she was crying; even now, it was useful to warn people about her moods. No one wanted to be near Aislin when she was truly upset. She was so in tune with the rock that had been used to construct the castle that even the walls and floor shook in sympathy.

As hot tears stung her eyes, Aislin wiped them away with the back of her hand. Red eyes just wouldn't do! She had to say goodbye to her father, and he would see that she had been crying. The king had enough to worry about without worrying about her, too. Even a fairy as powerful as King Carrigan had to keep his wits about him when traveling all the way to Fairengar.

Aislin walked to a table, taking shuddering breaths and clenching her hands into fists while the floor continued to vibrate. "Are you all right?" Twinket asked, still holding on to the chair leg.

"I will be in a minute," Aislin replied as she poured water from a pitcher into a crystal bowl.

When Aislin was first old enough to understand her power, her grandparents had tried to teach her to control her emotions. When she turned four, she was still prone to lose her temper, so her pedrasi grandmother gave her the crystal bowl and showed her how to focus her energy and use it to calm herself. She learned that washing her face in the water from the bowl could soothe her anger. Everyone in the royal household was delighted when it worked.

The water felt cold as Aislin scooped it up with her hands, but it was just what she needed. Her agitation faded as she splashed water onto her face.

Twinket sighed with relief when the floor stopped shaking. "Let me help you find your good luck charm. It's small and green, isn't it?"

Aislin nodded. "The leprechauns gave it to me. It's a charmed emerald and—wait, I think I know where it is!"

Running over to a table beside her bed, she opened the lid of a small box. "I found it!" she declared, and stuck the oval stone in her pocket.

There was a knock on the door. Aislin turned toward the sound. "Yes?" she called as the door opened.

"Your father is about to leave," an ogre footman named Skarly told her.

Aislin started running. "Thank you!" she called as she dashed past him out of the room and down the stairs. Passing a window, she heard the sound of the fairy knights' horses stomping impatiently in the courtyard. When she threw open the door, light from the torches lining the walls reflected off the silver armor of the fairy knights lined up behind her father's stallion, Wind Racer, nearly blinding her. She blinked, waiting for her eyes to recover. When she could see again, she spotted her mother, Queen Maylin, kissing her father while Timzy waited for his turn. Not wanting to miss saying goodbye, Aislin hurried down the stairs.

She had just reached her father's side when Wind Racer stomped his feet, forcing her to take a step back. She had been brought up riding the gentle ponies bred in the pedrasi mines, and while she admired the fairies' fiery-tempered horses, she had no desire to ride one herself.

Her father saw her and drew her in for a warm hug and a kiss on her cheek. Taking the charm from her pocket, she handed it to him, saying, "Please keep this with you for luck."

He smiled and patted her cheek. "I will," he vowed, tucking the stone into his own pocket.

A moment later, he'd mounted his horse and was raising his fist to signal that the troop was moving out. Aislin stepped aside as Wind Racer led the way over the cobblestones. Joining her mother and Timzy on the steps, she watched the fairy knights leave. Aislin counted them as they rode under the portcullis. Her father was taking all the knights stationed at the castle with him. That fact alone was enough to make her worry.

"Did you learn why Father was summoned?" Aislin asked when the last knight was out of sight and her mother had turned to go inside.

Queen Maylin nodded. "The messenger told us. Join me in my solar and we'll talk. It's time for Timzy to go to bed."

"But Mother...," Timzy began.

"I let you stay up this late so you could say goodbye to your father," said the queen. "You are not staying up any later."

By the time they'd sent Timzy to his room and had reached the queen's solar, Aislin was bursting with questions. A bright, cheery space with more windows than most rooms in the castle, the solar was the princess's favorite. There was no one there when they arrived, no ladies-in-waiting ready to cluster around the queen or minstrels ready to entertain her. Unlike the fairy royalty, pedrasi like Aislin's mother (and her maternal grandmother, Queen Amethyst) didn't believe in royal formality in their everyday lives. Thankfully, this meant the solar was one place where they wouldn't be interrupted; it was a good place to speak in private.

Mother and daughter headed toward the window seat, where they could see out over the forest. "You must tell me what the messenger said!" Aislin began.

"He told us that someone has been trying to open the northern passes and that humans had been spotted near the Magic Gate," said the queen.

"They can't open the gate, can they?" asked Aislin, alarmed. "I was always told that Grandmother and Grandfather used the very best spells on it."

"It's true that humans can't open it, but the fact that anyone is there means something unusual is going on in the human lands."

"Please tell me all you know about the gate again," said Aislin.

Her mother gave her a tired smile. "When the fairies decided that it was time to leave the human lands, they came here to see my father. Once he gave them permission to make their home in the great forest, he helped your fairy grandparents, King Darinar and

Queen Surinen, create the gate using enormous boulders and powerful warding spells. No one has been able to pass through that gate since. Only the eagles that fly high between the mountains are able to go to the human lands to report back to the fairy king and queen. Perhaps the eagles have seen something, but we won't know anything more until your father comes home to tell us."

"I hope he comes back soon," Aislin said, turning to look out the window at the darkened forest.

"So do I," said her mother. "More than I can say."

Chapter 3

EVERYONE IN THE CASTLE was used to seeing Twinket accompany Aislin on her excursions out of the castle into the surrounding forest. The day after the king left, she joined Aislin, Poppy, and their friend Bim as they headed out to go mushroom hunting. Twinket rode in Aislin's basket while Bim rode in Poppy's.

When the group reached the meadow beside Blue Lake, they spotted tiny fairies flying around with freshly picked mushroom caps on their heads. "Where did you find those?" Aislin asked one as she passed.

"I'll show you!" the fairy replied. "We heard you were coming, so we saved you some. There were oodles out here today."

Aislin knew all about mushrooms. When she was

little, the fairies had taught her which ones were safe to eat and which ones she should never touch. Just because some were pretty didn't mean they weren't dangerous, and some of the most boring-looking mushrooms were the most delicious.

The fairy fluttered ahead, leading the way around the edge of the meadow to an ancient grove of oak trees. Mushrooms dotted the ground between the roots. As she drew closer, Aislin spotted more tiny fairies peeking out from under their new mushroom caps, adjusting them so they fit just right. Seeing the princess, the fairies darted into the air in streaks of color, swirled around her long enough to say hello, and flew off into the woods.

Aislin and her companions were busy picking mushrooms when Timzy and his friends appeared, racing toward them from the far end of the meadow. The children laughed and shouted as they ran, and Aislin knew right away that they were playing one of her favorite childhood games—Magic Gate. It was a game in which "fairies" fled the "humans" until they had reached the magic gate; this time, it was a mulberry tree where someone had tied a scrap of red cloth.

The game was so popular in part because it was based on something that had really happened in the fairies' history. For as long as anyone could remember, the fairies had lived side by side with the humans, trying to stay friendly, but avoiding involvement in their wars and conflicts. When distancing themselves became increasingly difficult, King Darinar and Queen Surinen decided that the fairies needed to move somewhere that the humans couldn't find them. The pedrasi king and queen, rulers of the land under the mountains, were happy to have them as neighbors. Once the fairies had moved to their new kingdom, the gate was sealed using powerful magic. Fairies and pedrasi can live for a very, very long time; hundreds of years had passed during which the fairies enjoyed their isolation and hoped that the humans would either forget them or come to believe that fairies were a myth.

A pedrasi child screeched and ran past Aislin. The children looked as if they were having so much fun that Aislin was tempted to join them, and she might have if she hadn't promised Cook that she'd bring back mushrooms.

Bim had no such reservations. "I'll play, too!" the little sprite cried when he saw that other sprite children were playing.

"Aren't you going to collect mushrooms?" Poppy asked him.

Bim looked down at his empty basket, then at the mushrooms. With a twitch of his fingers, a mushroom flew into the air and landed in the basket. "Here," he said, handing the basket to Poppy. "I've done my share." With a wave of his hand, he scampered off to join the game.

Poppy glanced at the plum-sized basket. She sighed and shook her head. "One mushroom! I don't know why we invited him."

"Because he's our friend," said Aislin. "We always invite him."

The number of children living in the castle was growing. For a long time, fewer and fewer babies were born to pedrasi and fairies every year. Children were precious to both groups, but they were becoming increasingly rare. When the daughter of the pedrasi royals married the son of the fairy royals, the newlyweds kept their union secret until they learned that they were about to become parents themselves. Hearing that their children had married without permission, the pedrasi and fairy royal couples were furious, but nothing could have softened their hearts faster than the news of impending grandparenthood.

They gave the southern tip of the vast land between the mountains to the new parents, making them rulers of their own kingdom. King Carrigan named it Eliasind, a fairy word for strength. Now couples with children gravitated to Eliasind, where every sort of fey was welcome. Aislin had friends as tiny as six-inch-tall Bim and as big as Igbert and Salianne, the giant brother and sister who lived with their parents in the deep woods. It wasn't unusual to find children of all sorts playing together.

Aislin looked up when she heard a shout. The younger children were darting this way and that, trying to avoid their pursuers. Aislin's basket was half-filled when Timzy and five of his friends raced past, heading for the other end of the meadow. Two sprites and a little pedrasi child were chasing them, shouting, "You can't get away from humans!"

"Run, Timzy!" screamed Twinket.

Aislin grinned. With two sprites on the "human" team, the others didn't stand a chance. Sprites loved to cheat. Their motto was "whatever works." Then again, sprites weren't the only ones who didn't always follow the rules. Suddenly a troll appeared in the middle of the field, growling and slobbering and making the "human" children stop in their tracks. The glamour lasted only a few seconds before it faded away, leaving

Peatie, one of Timzy's fairy friends, holding his stomach as he bent over, laughing.

Aislin and Poppy watched the children turn on Peatie and chase him around the field. Twinket tugged on Poppy's hem. "I think someone wants to talk to you," she said, and pointed into the woods.

A doe with soft, frightened-looking eyes was standing only a few yards away, pawing the ground nervously. Her speckled fawn stood behind her, its thin little legs shivering with fear. The doe made some high-pitched sounds that didn't mean anything to Aislin, but Poppy nodded and answered back.

"What did she say?" Aislin asked, irritated at the flash of jealousy that her friend could talk to animals while she couldn't.

"Tawny Coat says that there's danger in the woods and everyone must flee!"

"What kind of danger?" asked Aislin.

The fact that she had to wait for Poppy to ask the deer the question and wait even longer for a reply made her irritation grow. "People with weapons!" the fairy finally told her. "They hurt Sure Foot and the rest of the herd ran away. Tawny Coat thinks that the people are going to eat him!"

Aislin frowned. Neither fairies nor pedrasi killed or ate animals; they found the very idea repugnant. Whoever these people were, they weren't the normal kind of fey, if they were fey at all. "Where did she see them?" she asked Poppy.

"Near the big rocks in the pass," her friend eventually replied. "They don't look or smell like any creature she's ever seen before. She's going to warn the others." The doe and her fawn turned, their tails flicking as they bounded into the woods.

Aislin handed her basket to Poppy. "Please take the young ones and return to the castle. Tell my mother that there are hunters in the forest."

"Where are you going?" Poppy asked her.

"To learn more about them," Aislin said. "Father always says that you need to know the truth about something so you can make the right decisions. We won't know what to do until we know what we're facing."

"You should return to the castle, too, Princess! One of the guards can go," said Poppy. "Or let me go! I can fly there and back before the hunters notice me."

Aislin shook her head. "My father won't ask anyone to do something he won't do, and I won't either. And what if someone saw you? We don't know anything about these hunters, and I don't want them to know anything about us if we can help it. The last thing we want is for them to see fairies flying around. Please spread the word that everyone should keep out of sight."

"But what if they see you?" asked Poppy.

"I'll be careful," Aislin told her. "I can be just as silent in the forest as you. Please take the young ones home now. I'll see who these hunters are and hurry straight back."

Timzy had seen them talking and came running over. "What's wrong?" he asked. "You look so serious."

"There are hunters in the forest," Poppy told him. "Take everyone back to the castle. Aislin and I are going to investigate."

"But I—" Aislin began.

"Can't go by yourself," Poppy told her. "Hurry, Timzy. Go home and tell your mother about the hunters. Aislin and I will be right behind you."

When Timzy ran off to collect the other children, Twinket grabbed hold of Aislin's gown, saying, "I'm going with you, too!"

Aislin sighed. "Fine, but no one else! The more who go, the harder it will be to be sneaky."

Timzy was already herding the younger children back to the castle as Aislin picked up Twinket and started toward the pass. The princess had been there once before when she'd been out riding with her family. Huge, slick-sided boulders filled the narrow opening, too tall and smooth for anyone to climb. Even if the boulders hadn't been there, the magic wards placed on the pass would have made it impossible for anyone to get closer than a hundred yards. And this wasn't even the Magic Gate! Her father had told her that the gate filled a much bigger gap leading into the mountains, and had magic so powerful that it looked to outsiders as if there had never been an opening there at all. After closing the gate, the fairies and pedrasi had closed all the other passes as well, including the one located in what came to be called Eliasind. Aislin couldn't imagine who the hunters might be, or why they were near the pass.

Years of moving quickly and silently through the forest had made Aislin and Poppy able to sneak up on even the most vigilant of creatures. They had often surprised deer, quail, and the occasional dragon, so creeping through the forest without alerting the hunters was easy. Even if they hadn't been so quiet, however, the hunters were making so much noise themselves that they probably wouldn't have noticed them. Aislin could already hear them when they were still far off, breaking branches and snapping twigs in the forest and kicking rocks and pebbles as they splashed across streams. She knew that they were riding horses, too, and that the animals hadn't been trained for stealth. More than once she heard the horses call out to each other, announcing their presence in the forest; the mounts of fairies and pedrasi normally kept silent.

"Even the giants are quieter than these people," Poppy whispered to Aislin.

"Maybe they're not trying to be quiet," said Twinket.

While searching for the hunters, the friends stopped now and then so Poppy could warn the animals they encountered about the approaching danger. After hearing their warning, a family of porcupines scuttled into the underbrush, a unicorn galloped off, and a wild boar rounded up its children. Only the bear enjoying a newly discovered beehive seemed unconcerned. Sharp Claw, one of the biggest bears in the forest, grumbled his thanks to Poppy. When the fairy turned away, she told Aislin, "He said he'll go as soon as he finishes his honeycomb."

"They'll be here soon," said Aislin.

Poppy shrugged. "You can't move a bear who doesn't want to be moved."

A little farther on, Aislin realized that the hunters

37

were approaching them on a deer trail that meandered through the forest. Slipping into the thicker underbrush, the three friends hid so they could watch without being seen. Aislin studied the hunters as they passed by in single file. They were all men, coarser looking than fairies and taller than pedrasi. Their horses were big and solid-looking, not at all like the sleek steeds of the fairies or the pedrasis' small, sturdy ponies. Aislin covered her mouth with her hand when she saw a horse walk past carrying a dead deer slung over its back. She recognized Sure Foot, a young buck she had known since his birth.

"I feel sick," Aislin whispered when the hunters were well past. "They're killers and they flaunt it! Who do you suppose they are?"

"You mean 'what do you suppose they are,' don't you?" Twinket whispered back. "They aren't fairies and they aren't pedrasi."

"They smell funny, too," said Poppy.

A sudden thought made Aislin shiver. "Do you think they might be humans? I've never seen a human before. Maybe this is what they look like."

Even in the deep shade, Poppy's face looked pale. "I bet you're right," she replied. "We need to go home and tell everyone."

"We will, but first I want to make sure that Sharp Claw left," Aislin told her. "He should have run off by now, but I bet he's still at that old tree."

"We already warned him once," Poppy said. "Do you really think we need to warn him a second time?"

Aislin shrugged. "I hope not."

They slipped past the hunters, who were still picking their way through the forest on the deer trail. Once they had left the hunters behind, they began to run, and soon found Sharp Claw still digging into the honeycomb. Poppy gestured toward the deer trail while she talked to him.

Sharp Claw gave his paw one last lick. Dropping onto all fours, he turned and grumbled at Poppy. As the bear started to amble off, Poppy told Aislin, "He says he's not afraid of them and that he's bigger and stronger than any puny humans."

"He doesn't need to be afraid, just smart," Aislin replied. "Quick, let's climb up and watch for the hunters from the tree. I want to make sure they leave and don't get Sharp Claw."

Twinket held on to the folds of Aislin's dress as the princess began to climb. Aislin was halfway up the tree when she stopped to look around. The deer path led through thick underbrush, with closely spaced trees on either side, and opened into a meadow carpeted with wildflowers. She couldn't see the humans, so she glanced up at Poppy, who had climbed higher in the tree and could see even farther. "Where are the hunters now?" she asked.

"I can't see them," Poppy told her. "They're behind some pine trees and...They're almost here! Quick, climb higher!"

Instead of climbing, Aislin said, "Tell Sharp Claw to run. If the hunters see him, they'll kill him like they killed Sure Foot!"

When Poppy called out, the bear huffed and started to run. Seconds later, the men burst from the trees. A richly dressed man was leading the way, and when he spotted the bear running through the meadow, he dropped the reins and reached for his bow and arrow. Taking aim, he let the arrow fly, hitting Sharp Claw in the shoulder.

Sharp Claw staggered and turned back to the humans. Rising up on his hind legs, he roared so loudly that the tree branches shivered and leaves showered the forest floor. Shaking his massive head, the bear dropped back on all fours to charge the horse and rider.

"Go straight home and tell my mother everything you saw," Aislin rushed to tell Poppy.

"What about you?" Poppy asked her.

"I need to stop something very bad from happening." She dropped from the tree.

The horse was rearing as the human let go of his bow and grabbed for the reins again. With the other riders crowding from behind and thick forest on either side, the horse had nowhere to go. Gritting her teeth, Aislin landed between the horse and the oncoming bear.

"No!" the princess shouted at Sharp Claw, her back to the terrified horse.

She wasn't sure at first if Sharp Claw was going to stop, or even understand her, so she picked up a stick and threw it at him to get his attention. The stick hit him on the nose. Blinking, he slowed and finally noticed her standing in front of the horse, holding up her hand. The bear shook his mighty head. Roaring one last time, he turned and ran into the forest.

Aislin spun on her heels to face the still-plunging horse and watched as the rider was finally able to get it under control.

"You're either the bravest or the most foolish

girl I've ever met," the man said, walking his horse toward her.

Aislin edged away from the tree so the man wouldn't notice Poppy. "I didn't want anyone to get hurt," she replied.

"You're lucky *you* weren't hurt," said the man. "That bear could have ripped you to shreds!"

"Are you all right, Your Majesty?" one of the riders asked, coming up behind him.

He's a king? thought Aislin. *Then what's he doing here?*

"I am, thanks to this young lady," the king replied. "What is your name, child?"

"Aislin," she said, then wished that she hadn't told him.

"We were hunting for game, but neither my horse nor I was expecting a bear of that size," said the king. The man was very handsome in a rough sort of way, but his eyes were cold and seemed predatory, even when he smiled. As the other hunters joined him, they moved to encircle Aislin. "We weren't expecting people here either. It looks as if the land between the mountains is full of surprises!"

Chapter 4

AISLIN WAS STARTLED WHEN one of the riders moved his horse closer and grabbed her, pulling her up behind him. "You can't do this!" she cried, struggling to get down.

"If you don't sit still, I'll toss you over the back of this horse and tie you on like the deer," the man said, nodding toward Sure Foot.

Aislin gulped and stopped wiggling. She'd never get away if they tied her up! There had to be something she could do.

"Tell me where you live, girl," said the king. "I want to speak to your parents."

"My home is far away," Aislin said. "It's really hard to find."

The man smiled, but he didn't look at all friendly. "Then it's good that we have you to show us how to get there. Do we go north or west, child? All you have to do is point."

"You go that way," Aislin said, pointing back the way they had come.

"Why don't you want me to find your home? Do you have something to hide?"

"My parents don't like company," Aislin told him.

"I just want to tell them that their daughter saved my life," the king said. "I'll reward them if you'll tell me which way to go."

Aislin shook her head, her lips tightly pursed. Somehow, she didn't think that was all he wanted.

The man she was sitting behind looked over his shoulder to scowl at her, but the king just laughed. "She's a stubborn one," he said. "Just like my daughter." His eyes fell on Twinket, still clutched in Aislin's arms. "And apparently wealthy, unless this kingdom is so rich that even peasants can afford dolls with amethyst eyes. You interest me, Aislin. If you won't tell us where you live, we'll have to find it ourselves. Craiger, climb that tree and tell me what you see."

A man with long, red hair nodded and slid off his

horse. They all watched as he shimmied up the tallest tree, disappearing into the branches overhead.

Aislin held her breath, worried about what he might see. There was the castle, of course, but there was also so much other magic in these woods! What if a fairy flew past, unaware of the need to hide? Or what if the man spotted a sprite perched on a hawk's back? Or even a nymph, waving to her neighbor in another tree? Although news spread quickly among the fey, some might not yet have heard that there were humans in the woods.

For Aislin's entire childhood, she had heard stories about humans. Her nursemaid, Larch, had told her and Poppy about the awful, scary things that humans did. These tales were enough to prevent the children from wandering off at night, or ever consider trying to find a way out of the mountains. Keeping the secrets of her magical kingdom was so engrained in Aislin that just hearing of humans infiltrating the land was a nightmare come true. And here she was, caught up in the middle of it!

Leaves rustled and the man's feet reappeared. "I saw a castle," he told the king, even before he reached the ground. "It's bright white with pennants streaming from every tower. We go that way."

Aislin's heart sank when he pointed toward her home. She would have had a better chance of leading the men astray if one hadn't actually seen the castle! Even so, it was going to take them a while to get there, which might give her family a chance—if only she could get a message to them.

She was worried about her mother and Timzy. From what Aislin had seen of the humans, it was clear she could pass for a human herself. But her mother was very obviously a pedrasi, and Timzy looked like a full fairy except for his rounded ears. Anyone who spotted them would know immediately that they weren't human. Letting humans know that fey lived between the mountains was exactly what her family had been trying to avoid.

Aislin wouldn't have been so worried if her father had been home. He could have created a convincing glamour to make the humans return the way they had come. Unfortunately, no one else's magic was that strong, and their glamours often fell apart. What made it even harder was the fact that they couldn't use more ordinary magic for fear of revealing the truth about themselves. Without her father there to cast a glamour, the castle's inhabitants would have to find another way to send the humans packing.

Aislin wondered if she could use her capture to her advantage. Maybe she could get the humans so lost or confused that they couldn't find the castle. Even if that wasn't possible, any way to delay their arrival would be helpful. The first thing she'd have to do would be to get word to her mother that the humans were on their way.

As they rode through the forest, Aislin waited for just the right moment. When the men were distracted talking among themselves about how to get around an impenetrable thicket, she held Twinket up to her mouth and whispered, "Go home and tell my mother to hide everything and everyone who is obviously fey. The humans are coming, and I don't think I can stop them."

A few minutes later, the path angled through thick underbrush. When Aislin saw that no one was looking her way, she dropped the doll and watched her scurry off into the woods.

The deer trail disappeared at the edge of a stream. Craiger rode ahead a short way, then returned to say, "I suggest we follow the stream. It appears to lead to that castle."

"Is Craiger right?" the king asked Aislin.

"I can't say," she replied, although she knew that the stream changed direction in just a little while.

The forest was thick on both banks, so the men walked their horses into the water and headed upstream. The man who'd grabbed Aislin dismounted, but when she tried to get off as well, he ordered her to stay. Thankfully, as the men focused on walking their horses across the slippery rocks, she was the only one who noticed the water nymph peeking out at them from under a clump of water lilies. She was also the only one who noticed the tiny fairies glaring at them from the iris blossoms that edged the stream. Aislin was so afraid that the men might spot the magical creatures that she held her breath each time they passed one, but they didn't seem to notice anything unusual at all.

It wasn't long before the stream meandered away from the castle, angling farther afield with each turn. After a short discussion, the men turned their horses around to retrace their steps, but the water was suddenly deeper and the current too swift for the animals to keep their footing. Aislin knew right away that the water nymphs were trying to help, but she was afraid the men would become suspicious if this went on too long. She was relieved when they left the stream and started looking for another way through the forest.

The group was following an old, faint trail through the woods when Aislin spotted tiny fairies peeking out from under rhododendron leaves. When a horse shied, she glanced down at the ground. A vine was creeping across the forest floor even as she watched.

"No!" Aislin shouted. The fairies looked confused, but they stopped making the vine grow.

"No, what?" asked the man in front of her.

Aislin caught herself, wishing she hadn't spoken out loud. "No, we shouldn't go that way," she told him.

"And why is that?" asked the man.

"Because that leads to a swamp," she said, then gave herself a mental kick. The swamp would have been perfect; they could easily have lost their way.

"Somehow, I doubt that you're really trying to be helpful," said the king. "Perhaps that's the way we *should* go. Ride on, gentlemen."

Aislin forced herself not to smile. If she was lucky, the men would get lost in the swamp and she could get away from them. Or even if they didn't get lost, getting stuck in the swamp would delay them, giving her mother time to get the castle ready.

A mockingbird landed on a branch near Aislin, cocking its head to look at her. When it flew off in a flutter of wings, Aislin was certain that the bird was reporting to the fey at the castle. She sighed, wishing once again that she could talk to birds so she could find out what was going on at home. Although her mother would have sent word about the humans to Fairengar right away, Aislin doubted that help could arrive any time soon.

Aislin knew news of the humans must be spreading when she saw ogres moving among the shadows in a darker patch of the forest. Instead of being loud and pushy as they usually were, they actually seemed to be hiding. If the humans saw ogres lurking in the woods, it would be as bad as seeing fairies flitting around, and Aislin wasn't about to let it happen.

She knew that the stubborn ogres probably wouldn't listen, even if she could warn them off, so she decided to try a different approach. As they often froze in place when she sang in the Great Hall, she knew it would work, but she couldn't sing one of her usual songs. It would have to be one that didn't include any references to fairies, pedrasi, or any other kind of fey. All she could come up with was a song for small children about a naughty bunny who was caught stealing carrots. Aislin put her heart into the simple melody. The ogres had been edging toward the riders, but at the first few notes they froze and went glassy-eyed. The horses kept walking, but the humans all turned to look at her.

Aislin sang the song through three times. By the time she'd stopped, they were well past the woods where the ogres were lurking and had reached the edge of the swamp.

"We appreciate the serenade, but I'd like to know why you sang just then," said the king.

Aislin shrugged. "I like to sing," she told him.

"And well you should," said the king. "You have the voice of an angel. I could listen to you every day. But right now, it occurs to me that you might be trying to warn someone of our approach. No more singing, understand?"

Aislin nodded. She didn't need to sing now. The ogres weren't likely to follow them into the Great Mud-Sucking Swamp.

"By my reckoning, the castle is in that direction," said Craiger.

Aislin looked where he was pointing. Craiger was right; the castle was straight ahead. If they hadn't had to go through the swamp, it wouldn't have taken them long to get there.

Aislin had to admit that the man was good at finding his way through terrain he'd never seen before. When they reached a series of shallow-looking pools, he stopped at the edge and shook his head. "I don't like the look of this water," he said. "We'll go around."

A younger man with a sharp nose and curly brown hair urged his horse forward. "You're overly cautious, Craiger. Do you see how shallow it is? I say we ride across and save ourselves some time."

He was moving his horse toward the water when the king said, "Halt! I trust Craiger's judgment. If he says we go around, then that is what we'll do."

Craiger turned to the younger man. "We won't go near this water for a number of reasons. First, notice how there is no plant life near the edge? Nothing is growing within two feet of the water. Second, there is nothing swimming in or on the water. If this was a normal pond, we should see fish in the water or insects on the surface. Either there is something we can't see living in this water, or the water itself is dangerous."

This man is smart and too observant, Aislin thought as the riders followed him around the edge of the pond. *He might be the most dangerous.*

Craiger kept the men to the narrow strips of land that divided one pond from another. Sometimes the land was fairly solid, but in other spots it was little more than slippery mud that made slurping sounds every time a horse lifted its hooves. The route Craiger chose switched back and forth across the swamp, ultimately leading to the far side where ponds and mud gave way to forest once again.

It was dusk by then, and growing dark under the trees. Unfortunately, the party was close enough to see a warm glow just above the treetops. Aislin knew that it was the setting sun reflecting off the white castle, something she normally thought was beautiful, but hated the sight of now. There was no turning the hunters aside, not with the castle itself showing them the way.

Chapter 5

ALTHOUGH AISLIN HAD HOPED that the castle guards would have raised the drawbridge, it looked just as it usually did, with the bridge down and two guards on either side of the portcullis. As far as she could tell, the only difference was that, instead of their typical fairy silver, the guards wore dull-gray helmets that covered their pointed fairy ears and bulky, padded clothes that concealed their slender fairy bodies.

"Who goes there?" called one of the guards.

"King Tyburr of Morain," replied one of the king's escorts.

A shadow moved inside the courtyard as someone ran to spread the word that a human king was at their gates. The guards beckoned the humans in, giving a nod to Aislin as they passed. She looked around as the horses clattered across the drawbridge and into the courtyard beyond. Unlike the normal bustle of activity, there was hardly anyone about. Even odder, she was surprised to see two figures standing at the top of the castle steps, dressed as the king and queen. Of course, neither of them were her parents.

Larch, the fairy nursemaid, was dressed as the queen. A white veil covered her pointed ears and a padded gown disguised her slender figure. Looking more closely at the pretend king standing beside her, Aislin realized it was Nurlue. Aislin didn't recognize him at first because he had shaved off his long beard—a real sacrifice for a pedrasi.

The humans seemed wary, keeping their hands on their swords while they looked around, as if they expected an ambush from any direction. The fake king and queen were smiling, however, and did their best to look pleased to see them. "Welcome to our home!" Nurlue exclaimed. "I am King Nurlue and this is my wife, Queen Larch." Though Aislin knew their true features, she was impressed with their disguises; Nurlue passed as a short human with a round body and a rather large nose.

"I am King Tyburr of Morain," said the human

king as he studied his hosts. "It is kind of you to welcome uninvited strangers. Not everyone would." He turned and nodded to the man who had lifted Aislin onto his horse. At pressure from the man's legs, the horse started forward. "We encountered this young lady in the woods. She saved me from an attacking bear. I would like to commend you on the bravery of your very special daughter."

Larch reached toward Aislin. "An attacking bear?" she asked, worry in her eyes.

This seemed to please the human king. When the horse stopped beside him, he leaned toward Aislin. "I wasn't sure you were a princess until just now. Your mother's concern is obvious."

Aislin made a strangled sound and slipped off the horse. She darted up the steps, where Larch caught her in her arms. Furtively, she whispered, "Be careful of the king and the man with red hair. They're both smart and observant."

Larch gave her a tiny nod. "Are you all right?" she whispered back.

"I'm fine," Aislin replied, and turned around to see one of King Tyburr's men leading the horse bearing the deer carcass forward.

"We did not know that we had entered your

kingdom and that we were hunting on your land," declared King Tyburr. "This buck belongs to you. I apologize for taking it without your permission."

Nurlue's smile faltered, but he quickly recovered and waved his hand, as if killing the deer didn't bother him at all. "Under the circumstances, such a mistake is understandable," he said, although he avoided looking at Sure Foot.

On an ordinary evening, fairy lights lit up the courtyard when darkness fell, but Queen Maylin seemed to have thought of everything. Fairies wearing helmets emerged from the lower castle doors to light torches placed in sconces on the walls. Aislin crinkled her nose at the smell, and Larch sniffed as if she too smelled something bad.

Nurlue glanced at the sky, then turned back to King Tyburr. "It is growing dark. Won't you join us for supper and a comfortable night's rest?"

King Tyburr smiled, although it wasn't warm or friendly. "We would be pleased to accept your gracious offer," he said, his hand still lingering by his sword. "We have traveled far with little to eat, and my men and I would appreciate a good meal."

King Tyburr dismounted, handing his reins to one of his men. Aislin backed away as he started up the steps. She waited while Craiger and the other men hurried after their king, then followed them to make sure that none were left behind to snoop.

The aroma of roasting food wafted from the kitchen, hurrying the hunters' steps. When they reached the Great Hall, the men were directed to seats at a table off to the side, while King Tyburr was escorted onto the dais with the royal family. A place had already been laid for him beside Nurlue, leaving Aislin to sit beside Larch. Aislin was relieved that there was no sign of her mother or brother, and that all the fairies were wearing some sort of disguise to cover their pointed ears and slender bodies. Sprinkled among the fairies were a few of the taller pedrasi, but none of them were seated near enough that the humans could inspect them closely.

A servant was pouring wine into their chalices when King Tyburr turned to Nurlue, remarking, "Your kingdom is very secluded and difficult to find."

"We like it that way," Nurlue replied. "It's peaceful here."

"Do you get many visitors?" asked King Tyburr.

Nurlue shook his head. "You're the first in a long time."

Or ever, thought Aislin.

58

King Tyburr took a sip of wine, and nodded his approval. "Do you ever travel beyond your borders?" he finally asked.

"Not in many years," Nurlue told him.

"And why is that?" King Tyburr asked.

"The rest of the world holds no attraction for me. I have everything I need right here." Nurlue patted Larch's hand.

The servants began to carry out platters and bowls filled with leafy vegetables, sautéed mushrooms, and root vegetables in heavy sauce. King Tyburr looked around expectantly, but when no other dishes emerged from the kitchen, he turned back to Nurlue. "I noticed that you have an abundance of game in your forest, yet you don't serve meat with your supper," he said.

Larch leaned forward to see past Nurlue. "We're careful about what we eat," she told King Tyburr.

"I can see why," King Tyburr said, glancing at Aislin before turning to the heavier pedrasi and the fairies' padded clothes.

Aislin blushed and turned away. She didn't know what he meant, but his tone of voice and the expression on his face told her that he was being unkind.

Noticing Aislin's pink cheeks, Larch pursed her lips. The fairy's hand shook when she reached for her chalice, causing her to spill wine onto the table. "How clumsy of me!" she exclaimed.

Aislin suspected that the nursemaid had done it on purpose to change the subject.

King Tyburr didn't seem to notice. "This wine is delicious," he declared, and drained his chalice. "I don't think I've ever tasted any like it."

"We make it ourselves," Larch told him proudly. "Our vintners are very talented. Be careful though— our wine can go straight to your head if you aren't accustomed to it."

King Tyburr laughed. "I'm sure I'll be fine." He smiled when a servant refilled his chalice.

Aislin thought the human king looked more relaxed than he had before. When she glanced at his men, they all seemed to be enjoying their food and wine as well. She noticed that the servants were quick to refill their cups with the potent fairy wine as soon as they were emptied. A few of the humans were already yawning. Only Craiger seemed more interested in the people around him than in what his trencher and cup held. He seemed especially intrigued by the fairies seated across from him. Aislin wondered if their disguises weren't quite good enough. When she looked at them more critically, she realized that one or two might have overdone it; although their bodies and padding-plumped arms were very round, their faces were still thin, and their hands long and narrow, making them look quite odd.

After sampling his food, King Tyburr turned back to Nurlue. "Most people don't believe that anyone lives between the mountains. I was surprised when I saw your daughter. Do you have many subjects?"

"A goodly number, scattered here and there," Nurlue replied, careful not to reveal too much.

Aislin's gaze wandered back to Craiger. The man was staring at King Tyburr as if hoping to catch his eye. Whatever he had to say to the king, Aislin had a feeling that she wouldn't like it. Perhaps it was time for another distraction. Setting down her knife, she turned to Nurlue and said, "I think our guests might like a song, Father. With your permission…"

Nurlue glanced at Aislin, then at Larch. When Larch gave him a tiny nod, he said, "Wonderful idea, my dear. We always enjoy your songs."

Aislin stood and faced the humans seated at the table below the dais. As she began to sing a song about love and valor, everyone stopped talking. She had thought this through and was careful to leave out the words "fairy," "ogre," "flying," "magic," "curse," and all references to incredible age. Her gaze wandered around the hall as she sang, and she saw her plan had worked; she watched as everyone, including Craiger, sat back to listen and sip from their cups of wine. Only the servants seemed alert, hurrying to replenish the guests' drinks.

Aislin sang until the wine had made most of the humans fall asleep with their heads pillowed on their arms. By the time King Tyburr himself slumped with his mouth open, only Craiger was still awake, although even his head was starting to droop. Aislin kept singing until Craiger was snoring into the remains of his supper. As soon as she was sure that he really was asleep, she turned to Larch and Nurlue.

"Come with us." Larch beckoned and led the way to the anteroom next to the Great Hall.

"Mother!" Aislin cried out when she saw the queen waiting for them. Running to the queen, Aislin threw herself into her mother's arms. "I'm so sorry I wasn't able to keep them from coming to the castle! When I saw that it couldn't be avoided, I kept them away as long as I could."

"You did well," her mother said, holding her close. "My dear, brave girl! I wish it hadn't been up to you to deal with these men. I'm very proud of you."

Relieved to see her mother, Aislin was bursting with questions. "Is Father coming back?" she asked.

The queen shook her head. "I sent word to him right away, but the fairy messengers came back to tell me that neither your father nor your grandfather are in Fairengar. No one knows where they are right now. We have to handle this ourselves."

Larch snorted and shook her head. "I still say we should have given those humans the toxic mushrooms. Humans aren't to be trusted."

"We weren't going to kill those men!" the queen exclaimed. "Tyburr is a king! Surely his people know that he came this way. If he doesn't return, they'll come looking for him. The last thing we want to do is start a war! We'll just send them back where they came from and reseal the pass when they're gone."

"Shouldn't we put them in bed for now?" asked Aislin. "We can't leave them in the Great Hall all night. Do you have rooms ready?"

"We do," said the queen. "They'll sleep in the west wing. We'll post guards to make sure they don't wake up and go wandering."

"After drinking all that fairy wine, those men will be out till morning," said Nurlue.

"I hope so," the queen replied. "For everyone's sake."

"Oh, they'll sleep all right. After the last one fell asleep, I cast a spell to make their slumber long and deep," Larch declared. "They won't wake before morning unless something extraordinary happens."

"You didn't!" the queen said, alarmed. "I told you to talk to me before you used any magic!"

Larch shrugged. "You weren't there and it needed to be done."

"No more magic unless I agree to it," the queen told her. "Do you understand?"

Larch looked meek when she bowed her head and replied, "Yes, Your Majesty."

"I've sent Skarly and Kwarel to carry the humans to their rooms," said the queen. "Aislin, come with me. I want to hear about everything that happened."

Aislin accompanied her mother to her solar, passing the ogre footmen on the way. Both ogres were carrying two humans, one over each shoulder. The humans were snoring loudly and didn't show any sign of waking.

"Poppy told me that a deer warned you about the humans and that you found them near the pass," the queen said as they reached the solar. "She also told me that she warned other animals, but Sharp Claw didn't listen. He was lingering when the king arrived and shot him with an arrow."

Aislin nodded. "Then Sharp Claw charged and I told him to stop. The king thought I had saved his life, but I was really trying to protect Sharp Claw. When the king ordered his man to take me up on his horse, he asked me where I live, but I didn't tell him. The man named Craiger climbed a tree and saw the castle. After that they knew which way to go. I tried to get them lost, but Craiger is too smart. He's as smart as the king—we have to watch them both. We also have to make sure that no fey show who they really are. The king and Craiger are sure to see it. When I was with the humans in the forest, fey tried to help me, but I told them to stop because I know how important it is that the humans don't learn the truth about us. The way Craiger was looking around during supper made me wonder if he doesn't already suspect something. I offered to sing to distract him."

"You have helped so much, my darling girl," said the queen. "I wish you hadn't had to talk to the humans at all. Thank you for everything you've done. Now go to bed and don't worry. I have something in mind that will make them want to leave."

Aislin hurried to her room, wondering what her

mother had planned. When she opened her door, Twinket ran to greet her.

"Princess, I was so worried!" cried the doll. "Did those horrible men hurt you?"

"Not at all," Aislin said as she scooped her up. "And Mother has a plan to make them leave in the morning. Thank you so much for helping me!"

"You know I'll always do whatever I can for you," the doll said, and planted a quick kiss on Aislin's cheek.

The princess sat on the edge of her bed and sighed. "I'm really tired and I have a feeling that tomorrow morning is going to be very interesting, but I don't think I'll get a wink of sleep knowing that humans are in the castle."

"I can go watch them for you," said Twinket. "If you go to sleep now, I'll wake you if something happens."

"I'd appreciate that," Aislin said, stretching out on her bed. She closed her eyes as the doll climbed down the covers and ran across the room. The princess was asleep before Twinket reached the door.

It seemed like only moments later that Aislin woke to Twinket patting her face.

"Get up! You have to come see this!" cried the doll. "There are ghosts in the castle and they're trying to wake up the humans!"

"Huh? What?" Aislin mumbled, still half asleep. "This castle doesn't have any ghosts!"

"The sprites invited them here. They're trying to scare the humans away!" exclaimed Twinket.

Suddenly wide-awake, Aislin slipped off her bed and ran to the door. "Go tell Mother and I'll try to stop them," she told the doll before starting down the corridor.

Aislin was out of breath when she reached the west wing, but she didn't stop until she spotted the guards at the end of the hall. They were arguing with a group of sprites who were snickering and peering toward the rooms where the humans were staying.

"What's going on?" she asked the guards.

"The sprites invited ghosts into the castle," said one of the guards. "Do you know how hard it is to get rid of those things? Once ghosts arrive, they never want to leave, and they make so much noise that no one can get any sleep. They won't give up until they either scare you or drive you batty."

"That's why we invited them here!" cried one of the sprites. "If they scare the humans enough, that king will leave and never come back."

"*Ooooh!*" wailed a ghost somewhere out of sight.

Aislin scowled and ran toward the sound. When she reached the corner, she saw three pale figures gliding from door to door, moaning. Cold fog drifted across the floor, seeping under the doors. The princess darted behind a tapestry covering an alcove and gave out a muffled shriek when she ran into Bim. The little sprite was peeking at the ghosts, chortling.

"Why are you doing this? My mother is going to make them leave," Aislin whispered.

"We want to help," Bim whispered back. "Look, one of the doors is opening!"

Aislin joined him in peeking out from behind the tapestry. Two humans stepped out of a room and looked around. A ghost floated toward them, waving its arms and moaning. The men fell back into the room, slamming the door.

Other sprites carrying lanterns began to creep along the corridor. Bim reached for an unlit lantern on the floor, whispering, "They started without me!"

As he was lighting it with his magic, Aislin asked, "What are you going to do with that?"

"Knock on the doors and lure the humans to the window and make them fall out," the sprite whispered.

"That's horrible!" Aislin said a little too loudly. "Stop this right now! Mother will be furious."

"She won't be mad if we get the humans to leave!" declared the sprite.

"Bim, I order you to stop!" Aislin said in a fierce whisper.

The little sprite sighed. "Oh, all right. If you're going to be like that!"

Dousing the lantern, Bim stepped out from behind the tapestry and went to talk to the other sprites. They gathered around him as he whispered furiously, pointing at Aislin, who had come out from behind the tapestry, too. The sprites looked disappointed as they put out the flames in their lanterns and started down the stairs. Soon only Bim and his father were left to talk to the ghosts, who seemed reluctant to leave. When the pale figures hesitated outside the doors, Aislin walked toward them. As they turned in her direction, she pointed her finger at the stairs and whispered, "Go, and don't come back!"

The ghosts moaned louder than before, but they all drifted past her and around the corner. Bim and his father followed, stopping long enough for the little sprite boy to whisper, "Don't blame us if the humans stick around."

"I won't, but I will blame you if those ghosts don't leave!" Aislin replied.

Queen Maylin and Larch were there when Aislin reached the first floor. "I was waiting until the small hours of the morning, but I think we need to take care of this now," said the queen. "Larch, please begin."

Everyone watched as Larch started walking. "What is she doing?" Aislin asked her mother.

"Sending a dream to the king that will make him think he is urgently needed at home and make him want to leave."

No one moved while they waited for Larch to return. She was back only a few minutes later, looking pleased with herself. "There! That should do it!" she announced. "King Tyburr may not remember the dream when he wakes, but the desire to go home will stay with him."

"Excellent!" said the queen. "Now everyone except the guards must go to bed and stay away from the tower. We should be rid of these humans in the morning!"

Aislin went back to bed, expecting to finally get some sleep, but it wasn't long before Twinket returned with more news. "One of the humans got up and went looking for the garderobe. A guard told him where it was, but just as he got there, Jasper came out."

Aislin gasped. "I forgot that a satyr lives in the west wing. What happened?"

"The lighting wasn't very good, so all the human saw was Jasper's shadow," said Twinket. "He ran away screaming something about a monster. Now Jasper is upset. You know how sensitive he is about his broken horn."

"What did the human do after that?" Aislin asked her.

"Nothing. He stayed in his room," Twinket replied.

Aislin sighed and burrowed back under her covers. "I hope nothing else happens!"

Exhausted, she fell back asleep, but jolted awake once more when Twinket returned. "Cosmo just had a bad dream. You could hear him roaring in his sleep all the way to the top floor. I went downstairs to wake him. He said he was dreaming that young humans were chasing him through a labyrinth with swords and spears! It sounded really horrible."

Cosmo, the Minotaur, lived in the lowest floor of the castle. He often had bad dreams and was very loud when he did.

"Did the humans hear him?" asked Aislin.

"They must have," said Twinket. "I could hear them talking, but none of them came out of their rooms. The sprites are watching them now."

Aislin was about to lie down again when a new thought occurred to her. "What do you mean when you say 'watching'? They didn't go in the humans' rooms, did they?"

"Of course not!" Twinket assured her. "They're peeking in through the windows."

"They shouldn't do that! The humans will see them!" Aislin cried.

"No, they won't," Twinket said. "It's so dark out they won't see a thing. Everyone is just trying to help, Aislin. You can't blame them for that!"

Aislin glanced out her window. It would be light soon. Maybe she could get some sleep after the humans left.

Chapter 6

THE RACKET IN THE courtyard woke Aislin shortly after dawn. Springing from her bed, she ran to her window to see the men shouting below as disguised fairies led saddled horses from the stable. King Tyburr was there, giving orders. A moment later, "King" Nurlue emerged from the castle.

"Are you leaving us so soon?" asked Nurlue.

"I thank you for your hospitality, but I'm needed at home and we must be off!" declared King Tyburr.

"If you must leave...," Nurlue began.

"Strange things go on in this castle," King Tyburr interrupted. "Two of my men claim they saw ghosts outside their door last night. Others swore that giants carried us to our beds. I believe them. It rained before dawn and I saw enormous wet footprints inside the door when I came down just now. I slept through the night, but I received reports of strange monsters in the hallways, and beasts roaring in the night. Three of my men saw tiny faces peering at them through the windows. I noticed myself that many of the people here are unnatural. No normal person moves as gracefully as a cat or smells like flowers when they sweat."

Aislin was practically hanging out the window, trying to hear what they said.

"I swear I've never seen ghosts or giants inside this castle," Nurlue told him. "Many of my people wear scented oils to make themselves smell like flowers. Your men must have been dreaming. Perhaps it was the wine."

"Your wine was indeed powerful and gave me the best sleep I've had in years, but I trust my men's judgment, and I know that things are not as they should be here," said King Tyburr. "I've half a mind to search your castle and purge it of the monsters before I leave. Perhaps I should stay one more day and make this place safe for your family, since you seem unwilling or unable to do so. I wouldn't make the offer, but your daughter saved my life yesterday, and I feel that I owe her this much. Craiger, tell the men we're staying to hunt down the monsters!"

Aislin gasped. If those men went looking for monsters, they were likely to find her family hiding just out of sight. The humans had to leave and they had to leave now! There was only one thing that would make them go, and she refused to take the time to really think about it. Throwing on an ordinary gown, she ran down the stairs to the courtyard just as the humans prepared to come back inside.

"Aislin, wait!" Poppy cried when the princess ran past. But Aislin scarcely noticed that her friend followed her.

"King Tyburr, please save me!" Aislin exclaimed as she ran out the door. "I can't stay here another minute. I'm so frightened in this castle at night. It's all right during the day, but at night the monsters come out and I have to lock myself in my room until dawn."

"Are you sure, child?" asked the king. "I can stay and slaughter the monsters. I swear we'll search every inch so there's nothing left to terrorize you and you'll be safe here in your own home."

"But the ghosts will still be here!" wailed Aislin. "You can't slaughter the dead. Please just take me with you. I want to leave right away!"

Aislin was indeed afraid, not of any monsters, but of how the humans could hurt the people she loved.

The fairies could use magic to stop them, of course, but then they'd be revealing the very thing they wanted to keep secret. Someone was bound to get hurt if Aislin didn't put an end to this now!

The men on the stairs stopped and turned back to King Tyburr.

"Please, Your Majesty," Aislin said to the human king. "Please take me away from here."

King Tyburr nodded. "Very well, dear girl. Craiger, we're going now. Have the men mount up. You, over there!" the king called to Poppy. "Go fetch the princess's things. Enough for two days' travel. I'll see that she gets all she needs when we reach my castle. You, go with her to make sure that she hurries."

Poppy looked horrified, but she turned and ran back down the corridor with one of King Tyburr's men behind her.

Aislin tried not to think about what she had committed herself to doing. But letting these men back inside might very well mean death for her family, who were so obviously not human. According to the old tales, humans often considered anyone who was different from them to be a threat. Who knew whom the humans would consider monsters now?

The men were leading a horse toward Aislin when

Poppy came back carrying a large sack. The scarf covering her head was askew, as if she'd put it on in a hurry. Aislin caught her eye and tucked her own hair behind her ear. Poppy understood and fixed her scarf while one of the men took the sack from her. When no one was looking, Poppy patted the base of her throat. Aislin glanced down. The mood stone was glowing bright red. Turning away from the men, she ripped the chain from her throat and clutched it in her hand to conceal the glowing color; she didn't want to show King Tyburr even that much magic.

"The maid should come with us as well," King Tyburr said, pointing at Poppy. Aislin hated to drag Poppy into this mess, but she couldn't help but be relieved she'd have a friend by her side.

But one last thing first. "I have to say goodbye to my father," she cried, and ran to Nurlue.

"Here, give this to my mother," Aislin whispered to Nurlue, slipping the mood stone into his hand.

"Do you want us to do something?" Nurlue whispered back. Aislin knew that he was talking about magic.

She shook her head, mouthing the word "no." "I'll be fine," she said out loud. After giving him a quick hug, she headed down the steps to the courtyard.

"As it happens, my son is looking for a bride," King Tyburr told her from astride his horse. "You're brave and have good sense, things that are sorely lacking in most of the young ladies he's met. You can meet him and see if you're suitable for one another. Now it's time to leave. We have a long ride ahead of us."

As the men hustled the two girls to the waiting horse, Poppy leaned closer to Aislin. "The man didn't think I was fast enough when I packed your bag. He shoved some things in, including Twinket."

Aislin nodded. She was leaving her beloved family behind, but at least she'd have some allies with her. A moment later, one of the men picked her up and set her on a horse. A second man plunked Poppy down behind her while another rider took the horse's reins. Then they started off, barely giving Aislin time to wave to Nurlue before they were passing under the portcullis and across the drawbridge. The king was in the lead again, with Aislin only a few horses back.

The group was just entering the forest when she turned around one last time to gaze at the castle glowing in the morning sun. She watched it for as long as she could, wondering if she'd ever see it again. Once the castle was out of sight, she rode with her head down, thinking hard. She'd wanted her mother to have the necklace so that the family didn't need to worry. As long as they could see the colors change, they would know that Aislin was all right. As far as she knew, it would work even from far away. But if she *really* didn't want them to worry, she would have to be as calm as possible. She knew her parents well; if she wasn't happy, her father would use whatever means necessary to get her back—even if it meant ending their centuries-old seclusion and revealing the fairies to the world again. Considering how important their reasons for leaving the human lands had been, she didn't want to be the one responsible for making them return.

Aislin turned around when she felt Poppy shaking behind her. "Are you all right?" she asked.

Poppy nodded even as she bit back a sob. "I'm fine," she said. "It's just that I've never been away from my family before. What will I do without them? What will they do without me?"

"We'll be back someday," Aislin said, trying to be reassuring.

"You don't know that," Poppy said, wiping her nose with the back of her hand. "We've both heard all the horrible things that humans can do. What if they eat us, or worse?"

"I don't think they'd do that!" Aislin said, even as she wondered what could be worse.

"But you don't know for sure!" Poppy wailed.

Aislin sighed and turned to face forward again. Apparently, she was going to have to worry about Poppy's happiness, too.

After that, Aislin was too caught up in her thoughts to notice where they were until they were actually entering the pass. It was a narrow opening that allowed only one rider at a time, and the horses were skittish about going in. Some were so frightened that their riders had to dismount and walk the animals through. One rider elected to ride through and had to fight for control of his mount the entire way. While the girls waited, Aislin patted the horse they were riding and Poppy murmured soothing words in the horse's language. When it was their turn, Poppy held tightly to the princess, and both girls were relieved when their horse walked docilely through the narrow pass.

Even if she'd closed her eyes, Aislin would have known the moment they left the kingdom behind. The forest air that had smelled so fresh and pure in the land between the mountains smelled stale on the human side. When she listened, the sound of birdsong seemed thin and flat to her ears. She looked around and noticed that the foliage wasn't as lush, or the green as intense as it had been at home. The more she saw, the more she realized that none of the colors seemed quite right, almost as if she was looking through a gray-tinted veil.

It was dusk when they came to a deep river where a large boat was waiting for them. The boat was big enough to hold all the horses and their riders, and the sailors waiting on board seemed happy to see the king return. Aislin and Poppy dismounted and boarded the boat, running to the rail to look over the side as soon as they were able. The water was murky, unlike the clear lakes and rivers they were used to at home.

When the boat set sail, the girls remained by the railing. As Aislin tried to gaze into the river's depths, she saw an occasional fish, but no sign of water nymphs or any other water beings. To her eyes, the river looked lifeless without the sparkle it had at home; she realized that the world of the humans was nothing like the land between the mountains. There was no magic in it, at least not as far as she could tell. Aislin felt truly homesick for the very first time.

Looking back the way they'd come, it occurred to her that the king had gone a long way to hunt, with a lot of unnecessary effort. *Unless,* she thought, *he hadn't gone to the land between the mountains to hunt game.* Gazing in the direction of the pass, she wondered if he had been looking for game at all, or something else entirely.

Chapter 7

POPPY BECAME SEASICK SOON after the boat started moving. Aislin tried to help her, standing at her friend's side as she was ill over the railing, and bringing water to rinse out her mouth. Although Aislin still had some things to learn from her mother about healing, she knew enough to calm a stomach. If only she'd had a stone to give her the strength...unfortunately, she didn't sense any nearby, and resolved to never travel without one again. After sailing downriver for the night and well into the next day, Aislin was relieved when they docked in a large, bustling port city.

As soon as the gangplank was in place, a man led Aislin off the boat and into a carriage. Another man hustled Poppy to a wagon where she was unceremoniously loaded aboard, along with trunks and sacks bearing the royal seal. The wagon took off, but Aislin had to wait in the carriage for another hour before King Tyburr joined her. The carriage had just begun to move when the king glanced at her and said, "Tell me, have you seen much of your father's kingdom?"

"I know the north very well, and the land around the castle," Aislin replied.

"What about the mountains to the south? Have you ever been there?"

"No, I've had no reason to go to the south," Aislin said, looking puzzled. "Why do you ask?"

"Just curious," said the king, and turned back to the letter he held in his hand.

Aislin didn't believe him for a moment. She doubted very much that the king did or said anything without a real reason. There had to be something other than vague curiosity to make him question her.

When the king didn't look up from his letter, Aislin turned to peer out the window, trying to take everything in. She had never seen anything like the human city before. Her first impression was that it was dirty and smelly. Stinking refuse clogged the gutters and dirty water trickled down the middle of the streets. A few intersections afforded her views of the gray-stone castle at the top of the hill, but as they drew closer, a high wall built of the same stone blocked her view. Closing her eyes, she reached out to the stone, finding comfort in its nearness.

After they passed through a heavily fortified gate, the streets were narrower and ran straight to the castle. Now that Aislin could see it better, she thought the castle looked cold and forbidding, as if joy and laughter were unknown inside its walls. She hoped she was wrong.

They were rumbling up to yet another wall when King Tyburr turned to Aislin and said, "I'll have my son come meet you as soon as you've settled in and gotten a few new things to wear. You will want to make a good impression, after all."

Aislin glanced down at her gown. It was simple, but nice. Although she had liked wearing pretty clothes at the fairy court, people dressed up in Eliasind only on special occasions, like birthdays or holidays. Perhaps meeting the prince was more of an event than she'd thought.

The princess looked out the window again as the carriage rolled to a stop. A group of men stood waiting for the king, and they converged on him as soon as he stepped out. He spoke to one, then another as Aislin waited for them to move aside so she could climb down as well. When King Tyburr finally walked off, one man remained behind to speak to Aislin. "Follow me," was all he said.

The man took her to another man, who looked her up and down, sniffing his apparent disapproval. From the way he was looking at her, she wondered if she had a stain on her dress or food stuck between her teeth. He started to walk away. When she didn't follow him, he turned back and said, "Aren't you coming?" in an impatient-sounding voice.

Aislin hurried after him then, certain that he must not be feeling well to be so irritable. The expression on his face had reminded her of her pedrasi grandfather when he had a headache. Aislin thought about it as the man led her up two flights of stairs to a door in a long corridor. "This will be your room," he told her, and turned to go.

Although Aislin thought the man was rude, she couldn't just let someone in pain walk away. She didn't dare take the pain away herself, knowing that it would reveal she wasn't human, but there were other ways to get rid of a headache. "Perhaps you'll feel better if you lie down with a cold, damp cloth on your head?" she said, giving him an encouraging smile.

His mouth opened and he gave her a dazed look. But before she could say more, the door flew open and Poppy was there. The fairy maid reached out and grabbed Aislin's hand, tugging her into the room. "Where have you been?" Poppy asked as she closed the door. "Twinket and I have been waiting forever!"

"I had to wait for the king," Aislin told her as Twinket ran up. "He told me that as soon as I get some new things to wear, his son would come see me. Where do you suppose I can get new clothes?"

"Maybe you have to buy them," said Poppy. "But we didn't bring any money with us."

"I could steal some for you," Twinket said as the princess picked her up.

Aislin laughed and set the doll on the bed. "I hope it won't come to that. Would you look at this room? It's awfully dark, isn't it?"

Although the room was large, it didn't seem very big. There was a huge bed covered with dark red hangings dominating the center of the space, a big wardrobe that looked almost black in one corner, two chunky, dark wood chairs, a small, matching table, and dark-colored tapestries on the walls. The floor was dark, too, and the two windows opposite the door seemed to let in very little light.

Poppy nodded. "What it needs is some fairy lights!" she said, raising her hand.

"Don't you dare!" cried Aislin. "Absolutely no magic while we're here! They can't know who we really are, and the surest way for them to find out is for you to use your magic. And you'll have to keep your ears covered all the time. Humans don't have ears like yours."

"What about me?" asked Twinket. "What should I do?"

Aislin turned to her and gasped. "I didn't even think about what humans would do when they saw you! You can't do anything, at least not where anyone can see you. You're only alive because of magic. Most dolls can't move on their own, so you can't either. And don't talk unless we're alone in the room."

"You mean I have to act like I'm dead?" Twinket said.

Aislin shook her head. "Not dead, just not alive. Be limp and quiet. You can listen, but don't move anything, including your eyes."

"I don't know how that's different from acting dead," Twinket grumbled.

There was a sharp rap on the door. Alarmed, Aislin glanced at Poppy and Twinket. The fairy maid quickly adjusted her scarf, making sure her ears were covered, while the doll flopped backward and let her arm dangle over the side of the bed.

"Yes?" Aislin called. "You may come in."

The door opened and a tall woman with gray hair piled on top of her head strode into the room, the expensive fabric of her gown rustling. When her gaze moved from Poppy to Aislin, her lip curled and she said, "Which one of you is supposed to be the princess?"

Poppy pointed while Aislin drew herself up to her full height. Even she couldn't think of a reason for the woman to be so rude. "I'm Princess Aislin, and you are..."

"Lady Speely. The king may say that you're a princess, but I'm not convinced. You don't look like a princess and no one has ever heard of your kingdom. Ah, well, it isn't for me to say. I'm here to make sure that you have everything you need. I understand that you didn't bring many gowns with you and will need more. I'll see that a seamstress comes to take your measurements right away." The woman turned to Poppy. "And this is your maid, I assume?"

The fairy nodded, keeping her eyes down.

"I suppose you'll have to do. You'll sleep on the floor in the adjoining room." Lady Speely pointed to a door in the far wall. "Someone will bring you a pallet."

The woman turned to survey the room and her gaze fell on Twinket. "Is that a doll?" she said, walking over to pick her up. "How odd looking, although it does have nice eyes. Aren't you too old for a doll?"

Aislin glared at the woman. "Not for that doll. Besides, the king's man packed her. I wouldn't have brought her if I'd had a choice."

Lady Speely smirked. "Apparently you aren't too old. You talk about the doll as if it was a real person. The ladies in the court are going to eat you alive!" She sounded pleased. "I'll be back soon with a seamstress. See that you're washed up before then. We'll throw out the gowns you brought with you as soon as the new ones are ready."

The door was scarcely closed behind Lady Speely when Aislin exclaimed, "What a horrible woman!"

Twinket sat up and made a disgusted face. "Hey, at least she didn't touch you! I need a bath!"

"And I'm supposed to sleep on the floor!" cried Poppy. "No self-respecting fairy sleeps on the floor! Inside a flower or on a spiderweb mattress, or curled up in thistledown, or even in a bed if you're in a cottage or the castle. But never on a floor!"

"If we were at home, the sprites would know how to handle her!" declared Aislin. "They'd stick her in a washtub and fill it with ants, and—"

The stone floor beneath them began to shake, making everything in the room quiver and rattle.

"Uh, Aislin, you need to calm down," said Twinket. "If you were wearing your necklace, it would be bright red. I wish you'd packed her calming bowl, Poppy. There's an old clay bowl on the table, but that's not nearly good enough."

"Why don't you think about something that makes you feel calm, like swimming in Blue Lake?" Poppy suggested.

"Or lying on a bed of moss in the woods eating blueberries," said Twinket. "You always like that."

Aislin drew in a deep breath and let it out slowly. "Okay, I can try."

She walked to the edge of the large, deep red rug

so that both of her feet were on the stone floor. Closing her eyes, she drew strength from the stone and thought about pleasant things, like floating on her back in the lake while watching small, fluffy clouds pass over her. As she became calmer, her heart rate slowed and the floor grew still.

"Thank goodness!" said Poppy. "I'm glad that worked."

"Tell me something, Poppy," Aislin said as she took a seat on one of the chairs. "When Lady Speely was here, why didn't you look her in the eyes?"

Poppy shrugged. "I'm trying to act like a human servant. I wanted to look meek."

Aislin frowned. "I don't know why. That woman acts as if she thinks she's better than us, but I know muskrats that are better than she is. You don't need to look 'meek.'"

"Oh, I think I should," said Poppy. "That way I don't have to look at her pickled face or her scrawny chicken neck!"

Twinket fell over, laughing. "Or her beady eyes!" she cried. The doll guffawed until her sides were heaving, but she suddenly stopped and sat up to look at Aislin. "Why did you say you wouldn't bring me? Don't you want me here?"

"No, I don't," said Aislin. "It isn't safe for you here.

I wish Poppy wasn't here either. I have a feeling that this place isn't safe for any of us."

Lady Speely was back only a short time later, ushering in a tiny woman carrying a reed basket. The little woman reminded Aislin of a sparrow with her small steps and quick movements, although her voice was surprisingly deep. While Lady Speely took a seat on one of the chairs, the seamstress set her basket on the bed and pulled out a measuring tape. Even while she jotted down measurements, the two human women kept up a constant conversation.

"I'll need more fabric for this one's gowns," said the seamstress. "I'll do what I can to make her look thin, but I can't work miracles. The styles today are meant for slender girls."

"Do you have *any* styles that would work on her?" asked Lady Speely.

"A few, and I'll try slimming colors, of course."

"I'll help you pick everything out," said Lady Speely. "I do enjoy that kind of thing."

"Wonderful!" said the seamstress around the pins she was holding between her lips. "You have such discerning taste."

"I prefer spring colors," Aislin told them.

Lady Speely laughed. "You would! Don't worry, dear. We know exactly what you need. Until the gowns are ready, I suggest you stay here. You'll make a very poor impression if you go out in the gown you're wearing now."

When the two women left a few minutes later, Twinket ran to the closed door and kicked it as hard as she could. Aislin could barely hear the little tap. "I hate that woman!" the doll declared.

"We all do," said Aislin. "I just hope they actually know what they're doing. What do you suppose the gowns will look like?"

"Nothing like the dresses the fairies make!" Poppy exclaimed. "Or pedrasi, for that matter. Instead of throwing out your old dresses, would you mind if I took them? I could alter them to fit me."

"You can have them once I have something suitable to wear. I don't trust those women to make choices for me. Now I'll have to make a list of pleasant things to think about. I have a feeling that I'm going to need it every time I see Lady Speely."

Chapter 8

AISLIN EXPECTED THE SEAMSTRESS to return with a gown or two the very next day. She was used to fairies whipping up a gown in a few minutes, and even pedrasi seamstresses never took more than a few hours. But the seamstress didn't return, nor did Lady Speely. In fact, no one else came by that day other than the servants who brought her meals and came to clean up afterward. When Aislin didn't receive word from the king, she began to wonder if he'd forgotten that she was there.

That evening, Poppy announced that there was no reason *she* had to stay in the room and she was going to go exploring. It was nearly midnight when she returned, bursting with things to tell Aislin.

"I went all over the castle, even some places I prob-ably wasn't supposed to go," said Poppy. "No one seemed to notice me as long as I acted like I was sup-posed to be there. This castle is big, but not nearly as big as Fairengar. It's not as fancy either, even if the humans who live here are really stuck up and think way too highly of themselves. When people think you're a servant, they act like you aren't even there. They say all sorts of things in front of you that they wouldn't say in front of each other."

"Do you know how to get out of the castle, in case it gets too awful and we have to run away?" asked Twinket.

Poppy nodded. "I know at least five ways, and two of them aren't through the castle gates. The humans have built secret passages all over this place, but I can find them as easy as slipping off a buttercup. Their eye-sight must not be very good if they can't see the clues that lead to hidden doors and secret panels. I almost walked in on the king and some men he was talking to in a room behind a secret door. I bet they didn't even know there was a listening hole in the ceiling above them, or another door in the corner. For people who like to be sneaky, they aren't very good at it!"

"Are there any secret doors into our rooms?"

Aislin asked, suddenly worried that someone might have been spying on them.

Poppy shook her head. "I already looked really carefully, and there's not even a spy peek-hole. I would have told you if there was anything like that," she said, sounding reproachful.

"What about the other places?" asked Twinket. "The ones where you're supposed to go?"

"I saw those, too. There's the Great Hall, which isn't very pretty, if you ask me. And the kitchen and the buttery and the armory and the throne room and the gardens and—"

"Tell me about the gardens," Aislin told her. "I'd like to go there."

So Poppy did, telling her about the beds of roses and lilies, hollyhocks and daisies, the small pond and the big fountain, the shrubs shaped like animals and the paths leading from one end of the garden to the other. The fairy described it in such detail that Aislin went to sleep dreaming about it that night.

Aislin was still hoping that the seamstress would bring the gown the next day, but by late afternoon she couldn't wait any longer. She had to get out and do *something*, even if it was just to stretch her legs. No one was in the corridor, so she slipped out of her room and started walking. When she turned the corner and finally did see someone, the man didn't give her a second glance. She followed him down the stairs, then turned toward the Great Hall.

Stepping inside the hall, she paused to look around, trying to remember what Poppy had told her. The hall was a big room filled with tables and a raised dais at the end, just like at home. Some of the tables were empty, but there were enough people sitting together while they talked, played dice, or ate a belated meal that the room seemed full. Aislin was surprised to see that many of them were soldiers wearing a griffin insignia on their tunics.

"*Go to the Great Hall, which you can't miss,*" Aislin recited. "*Go out the door farthest from the castle entrance, and turn right. Go past the metal suit, then out the third door to the left. The garden is straight ahead behind a wall.*"

"You sound lost," said a boy sitting at a table by the door. He set down the book he'd been reading and looked at Aislin with interest. He'd been so quiet that Aislin hadn't even noticed him. Seeing him now, she saw that he was a nice-looking boy with dark, curly hair and a friendly smile. Aislin thought he was probably around her age, if not a bit older.

"I am lost," she admitted. "There are two doors at

the end farthest from the castle entrance. I don't know if I'm supposed to take the one on the left or the right."

"If you're looking for the garden, you take the door on the left," the boy told her. "The door to the right will take you down the corridor to the throne room. You must be new here. I don't think I've ever seen you before."

"I am new," Aislin replied. "And all this is new to me."

The boy laughed. "It does take some getting used to. I have to admit that I got lost quite often when I first arrived."

"Have you been here long?" Aislin asked him.

"It feels like forever, but it's really been only a few months," said the boy. "That's more than enough, if you ask me. This place doesn't get any less overwhelming."

Aislin turned to look around. It was messier than she was used to, and didn't smell very good, but it wasn't any noisier or busier than her Great Hall at home.

"I don't mean the hall," said the boy. "You'll know what I mean after you get to know the people. Ah, I was waiting for someone and here he is. It was nice meeting you..."

"Aislin," she told him.

"I'm Tomas," he replied with a smile.

"There you are!" cried a handsome boy as he approached the table. "You're keeping us waiting. Come along before the girls start their walk without us."

"I'm coming," said Tomas. "Although I'd really rather stay here."

When he stood up, Aislin realized that he towered over the other boy. He was even taller than most fairies around his age, but where they were slender and wiry, Tomas was broad and muscular. Aislin liked the way he looked back at her as he walked away. She, too, wished that he didn't have to go.

After taking Tomas's advice, Aislin finally found her way to the garden. Although she was sure it was beautiful by human standards, she thought it was boring and much too orderly. A tall border of cypress trees ringed the entire garden. The flowers were planted in rows, the paths were straight, and the fountain was nice, but not nearly as lovely or interesting as a waterfall. When she started to explore, she discovered why the garden wasn't very big; the curtain wall surrounding the castle was only feet from the last of the cypress trees.

As Aislin drew closer to the stone wall, she sensed that something was wrong. At some point in its past, something big and heavy had hit it. *A siege engine, perhaps*, she thought, remembering her lessons about humans. Most of the fractures deep in the stone had yet to reveal themselves to the naked eye, but Aislin could sense that some were very close to the surface; so close, in fact, that pieces were about to break off.

Placing her hand against the wall, she closed her eyes and spoke to the stone. "Mend yourself," she said with a quiver to her voice.

Aislin could feel the faint vibration of fractures closing as the stone blocks made themselves whole again. In tune with the wall, she could hear the faintest sound of stone grinding against stone. Although she doubted that any humans could hear it, she knew that some animals could. She hadn't expected it to be a problem until she heard a mule bray and start to kick the weakened wall behind it. Even though she couldn't see them, Aislin could feel cracks race through blocks, spreading as the mule continued to kick. She tried to stop the cracks from growing larger, but there were too many to handle all at once.

Pressing both hands against the stone, Aislin could feel added pressure on the blocks as a man hurried down the steps from the top of the curtain wall to see to the mule. She felt when the fractures made the stone crumble beneath his feet. The man shouted as he began to fall. In a flash, Aislin drew strength from the mended stone and sent power to the weakened sections, making them shift and angle into a ramp that caught the man and allowed him to slide safely to the ground.

Aislin stepped away from the wall when she heard voices shouting. "Holstin, are you all right?" one asked.

"Just fine!" the man replied. "I can't believe that happened."

"It's a wonder you weren't hurt like Shilling was last week," said another. "I've never seen anything like this."

"Who tied a mule here?" someone shouted. "It should never have been tied this close to the wall."

"This wouldn't have happened if the stone hadn't been weak. We'll have to repair this section, too."

Aislin couldn't do anything about the broken blocks with the men standing there, but she could fix what they couldn't see. She set her hand against the wall again, and stood there until she was sure that all the fractures were mended and the fissures filled. When she finally turned away, Aislin decided that it was time to go back to her room. As far as she knew, no one could have seen her, but it was better not to take unnecessary chances.

Aislin had passed the fountains and had almost reached the garden's entrance when she heard people talking on the other side of the cypress trees. She soon realized that it was Tomas and his companions.

"Would you believe I actually found him talking to a servant girl?" the handsome boy was saying. "And she wasn't even pretty! Well, her face was pretty, but her skin was as tanned as a goat girl's and she was as plump as the cook's daughter."

"I think she's very pretty," said Tomas. "I like her just the way she is."

Someone snickered as if he'd actually said something amusing.

"Has anyone ever told you that you aren't a very nice person, Rory?" asked Tomas.

"Why would they?" Rory said with a laugh. "Few people would dare to talk to me like that. Besides, I'm a prince. I don't have to be nice."

"Actually, I think princes have an even greater need to be nice than people of lesser rank," said Tomas. "You have a responsibility to your subjects and you should show them compassion."

Rory seemed to think this was extra funny,

because he laughed loudly. The girls who were with him also found it amusing, laughing just as hard. Aislin counted at least three, although there could have been more.

"You say the most bizarre things, Tomas!" cried one of the girls. "I never know if you're trying to be funny!"

"I always mean what I say," Tomas replied, which made them laugh all over again.

Aislin hurried off then, not wanting to meet these people. They weren't very nice, laughing at Tomas and the poor servant girl like that. And if that was the prince, was he the one she was supposed to meet? He probably was, unless there was another prince in the castle. She'd have to send Poppy out to investigate more than just the castle's layout.

Soon after she returned to her room, a servant brought her supper with enough for Poppy as well. As soon as the servant was gone, Aislin turned to her fairy friend and said, "Instead of eating with me tonight, I want you to eat with the servants and see what you can learn about the people here. Find out how many are in the royal family and what they're like."

"But I was going to ask you about your walk!" said Poppy. "Did you see anything interesting?"

"I did," Aislin told her. "We can talk about that later. You can learn a lot from the servants and I think I should know about King Tyburr's family before I meet them."

"You're right," Poppy said, adjusting her scarf. "I'll see what I can find out. This might actually be fun!"

Aislin wasn't very hungry for the bland human food in front of her, so she only picked at it before getting up from the little table. She was preparing for bed when Twinket said, "It isn't fair! I wish you'd send me on an errand, too. I can go a lot of places at night."

"Maybe sometime, but you'd have to be really careful not to let anyone see you move," said Aislin.

The doll was clapping her hands when Poppy walked in, closing the door behind her. "What are you so happy about?" Poppy asked the doll.

"Aislin might send me on an errand!" she exclaimed.

"What did you learn?" Aislin asked her fairy friend.

Poppy grinned and took a seat on the edge of Aislin's bed. "A lot and it's all interesting. I went to the hall where the servants eat and they acted like I was one of them. It wasn't hard to get the maids talking. King Tyburr has two children. Prince Rory is his oldest. He thinks very highly of himself. His sister is named Selene. The servants say she used to be nice, but she hasn't talked to them since the day she surrounded herself with a group of nasty girls."

Aislin's heart sank. There was only one prince after all! The rude boy who had been talking to Tomas was indeed the prince she was supposed to meet.

"What about the queen?" asked Twinket.

"Her name is Queen Tatya. She's King Tyburr's second wife. His first wife was a commoner named Cloe. They say she was plump and pretty and really sweet. Everyone liked her a lot and the king was crazy about her. She died when Selene was four. King Tyburr married Tatya three years ago. She was a princess he met when he was traveling. The women I talked to said it wasn't a love match. They say she isn't very nice and that she complains about everything. She is also expecting her first baby soon."

"King Tyburr's family sounds awful!" cried Aislin. "I don't want to marry into a family like that!"

"Maybe we can go home soon," said Twinket.

"First I'll have to meet the prince. Then I'll talk to the king," said Aislin.

Early the next morning, when Aislin was still asleep, Lady Speely and the seamstress knocked on her door. When she didn't answer right away, the two women barged in and dumped the gowns on her bed. Aislin was struggling to sit up under their weight when Lady Speely went into the dressing room and emerged a minute later carrying Aislin's two old gowns. "You'll be expected in the Great Hall for supper tonight," the woman announced. "I suggest you wear your new yellow gown." With a swirl of her skirts, she was out the door, the seamstress right behind her.

The door had scarcely closed when Twinket cried, "Oh no!" and scrambled off the chair in the corner.

"What's wrong?" Aislin asked as the doll ran into the dressing room.

Twinket came out wringing her little hands. "Poppy is gone! That human took her!"

Aislin swung her legs over the side of her bed and slid to the floor. "What do you mean she took her?"

"Remember how Poppy didn't want to sleep on the floor? She's been getting little and sleeping in the pocket of your gray gown. She told me that the pocket lint was soft and warm and much better than an old, lumpy pallet."

"And Lady Speely took the gown!" Aislin cried.

"How are we going to get Poppy back?" asked Twinket.

"I guess I'll have to find Lady Speely and ask for the gowns," said Aislin. "I don't know where her rooms are, though. I'll just have to ask someone in the corridor and—"

The door opened and Poppy walked in, carrying the two old gowns. "Can you believe they were going to throw these out? These are perfectly good pedrasi-made gowns and better than anything a human could make. Just compare the size of the stitches!" She set the gowns on the bed beside the new ones.

Aislin was relieved to see her friend and more than a little surprised. "How did you get them back?" asked Twinket.

"I waited until they set the gowns in a pile to get tossed down the refuse chute," Poppy replied. "As soon as they left, I got big again and grabbed the gowns. You wouldn't believe the things they throw out in this place. Look at this!" The fairy held up a book with a torn page and set it on the bed beside the gowns.

"That's the book Tomas was reading yesterday!" Aislin exclaimed. "I wonder why he threw it away."

"Have you looked at your new gowns yet?" Poppy asked, examining the sleeve of the one on top.

"No," said Aislin. "I'm supposed to wear the yellow one to the Great Hall tonight."

"Yellow, huh? That would be this one," Poppy said, digging a gown out of the pile.

"Try it on, Princess!" said Twinket. "Let's see how it looks."

Aislin couldn't help but feel a little excited. Although she wasn't as clothes-conscious as some fairies, she liked getting new clothes as much as anyone. Poppy helped her put the gown on and settle it around her hips. When she glanced down, Aislin's excited smile disappeared and she gasped.

"That has to be the ugliest gown I've ever seen!" Poppy declared. "Why would anyone think that was pretty enough for a princess?"

"Maybe the seamstress doesn't know how to do her job," said Twinket. "And if Lady Speely helped her pick this color out, they both have awful taste."

The tension and worry that had been wearing on Aislin for the last few days suddenly took their toll on her. Covering her face with her hands, she burst into tears.

"Oh, Princess, I'm sorry!" Poppy cried. "I didn't mean *you* looked bad, just this awful dress!"

"I know I look horrible in it!" Aislin wailed through

her tears. "It makes me look like a daffodil is devouring me!"

The floor began to vibrate, shaking the furniture, and Aislin's hairbrush fell off the table with a clatter.

"Those stupid humans!" Twinket exclaimed. "I hate them!"

Aislin's chest heaved with a few ragged breaths and she sniffled. "They're not all bad. A few are actually nice," she said.

"When did you meet a nice one?" asked Poppy. "Some of the servants seemed nice enough, but you haven't talked to any of them."

"On my walk," Aislin said as she wiped away her tears. "I met a boy named Tomas who was very friendly." The shaking stopped as the princess thought about how nice Tomas had been and the way he'd smiled at her before walking away.

"I knew something happened on that walk!" said Poppy.

"What about the dress?" Twinket asked. "I say we have two choices. We can cut it up into little tiny bits and toss them out the window, or we can burn it in the fireplace. Either one would make us feel better."

"We don't need to destroy it," Poppy told her. "I was going to alter the gowns I brought back so Lady

Speely and the seamstress wouldn't recognize them. I'd be happy to change these, too. I was hoping that the seamstress had at least some talent, but apparently I was wrong. I learned a few things from my aunt. Let's see what we can do with this."

"That would be wonderful," Aislin said, and gave her friends a wobbly smile. "I'm sorry I got so upset."

Poppy shrugged. "We don't blame you. They haven't been treating you very well ever since we got here. At least we can do something about these dresses." Raising her hand, she pointed at the yellow gown. "We'll start with a softer shade of yellow." A sprinkle of gold shot from her finger, turning to glitter around the gown. The color changed from a harsh yellow to a buttercream color that looked pretty against Aislin's skin.

"Get rid of the bows, too!" Twinket said, tilting her head as she gave the dress a critical look. "And those horrible flounces."

More sparkling gold made the bows and flounces disappear. "And I'll change the lines of the gown a little," Poppy murmured.

When she was done, the gown was far more flattering and all three of the girls were pleased.

"Try on another one!" cried Twinket. "Let's see what Poppy can do with it!"

The girls made a game of it, trying to see which gown was the worst. Aislin thought it had been the yellow, but Poppy thought it was the bright pink. She turned it into a soft, muted rose that Twinket said was her favorite color. Twinket hated the ugly blue gown until Poppy made it the same shade as a robin's egg. They all liked the iron-gray gown after Poppy changed it into the color of a dove's wings. When they were finished, the girls were satisfied that Aislin would look her best.

Careful to keep Aislin's old gowns suitable for a maid and not too pretty, Poppy altered them for herself in no time at all. When she was done, the girls held their own fashion show, trying on their new gowns all over again, while Twinket modeled a scarf dress and one made out of a discarded ruffle. They danced to nonexistent music, collapsing in laughter when they were too tired to go on.

The girls were lying sprawled on the floor. Aislin sat up and looked around. With all the magic that had been used in the room, she couldn't help but notice that the room itself seemed brighter. Even the air smelled better, as if a fresh spring breeze had wafted away the stale, musty air. "I love what you did to the gowns, Poppy, but we need to be more careful about using magic. I think the human world looks the way it does because magic has been gone from it for so long. Bringing it back even a little bit might make some changes that people could notice."

"I'll be careful," said Poppy. "But I'll use magic whenever I need to if it will help my princess."

Chapter 9

P OPPY TUCKED ONE LAST lock of Aislin's hair into place and stepped back. "You look beautiful!" she said, smiling.

"You really do!" cried Twinket. "But you'd better go. I've already heard people in the corridor heading down to the Great Hall."

"Have fun!" Poppy said, walking her to the door.

Aislin gave her a half-hearted smile. "I'll be eating supper with the king and his family. I don't think there will be a lot of fun involved."

Aislin felt truly lovely as she made her way to the hall, certain that people were admiring her gown. When she arrived at the door, a servant escorted her to the raised dais, and announced, "Her Highness, Princess Aislin of Eliasind."

A beautiful young girl who Aislin assumed was the other princess was seated on the far side of the dais. Prince Rory was seated on Aislin's side with an empty seat between him and Tomas. Two empty chairs reserved for the king and queen were in the middle. Both the prince and Tomas stood at Aislin's approach. She was pleased when the servant indicated that she was to sit between the two young men; she was looking forward to talking to Tomas again. It was the prince who demanded her attention, however.

"Welcome to Morain, Princess Aislin," said Prince Rory. "I'm delighted that you could join us tonight! I must say, you look lovely in that gown. And your eyes... They're amazing!"

"Thank you," Aislin told him. "You're very kind."

As Aislin took her seat, she glanced toward the table below the dais where someone was making choking sounds. Lady Speely was staring at Aislin in surprise and her face was turning red.

"I thought you told the queen that you would take care of the girl's dresses!" exclaimed the woman seated beside her, in a voice that carried. "That isn't anything like the gown you described. It's prettier than most of mine!"

"I'm sure that isn't the same gown," Lady Speely told her. "The fabric isn't even the same yellow!"

Everyone seated nearby was listening to their interchange. As stubborn as her fairy relatives, Aislin wasn't about to let it go. "You must be mistaken, Lady Speely. This is the yellow gown that you wanted me to wear. My maid and I changed a few things, but you can't honestly think we changed the color!"

"I don't ... I never ...," sputtered Lady Speely.

Aislin turned to Princess Selene. "The ruffles and bows were a little much for my taste. I prefer my gowns to be simple and elegant, don't you?"

"Yes, of course," the princess replied, looking confused.

"Ah, here's my father and his lovely wife," said the prince.

Everyone in the hall stood as the king and queen entered the room. The queen was as round as Aislin's mother had been right before Timzy was born. When King Tyburr sat down, everyone waited until he nodded before sitting as well. After greeting his children, he turned to Aislin and said, "Good, I see you have a new gown. I trust you've been made to feel welcome."

"Yes, thank you, Your Majesty," Aislin replied. "Lady Speely has been particularly accommodating."

"Excellent!" he said, and searched out the servants waiting at the edge of the room. As soon as he beckoned to them, some servers hurried to the royal table carrying heaping platters while others made their way down the long tables, offering food.

Queen Tatya smiled at Aislin, but the smile didn't reach her eyes. "I'm delighted you're able to join us, my dear," she said. "The king told me about the horrible castle where you lived and how you had to leave in such a hurry. I thought you weren't able to bring much with you. How were you able to fit that gown in your bag? It's lovely."

"I didn't bring this with me," said Aislin. "Lady Speely had it made for me here."

"Really?" the queen replied. Raising one eyebrow, she glanced at Lady Speely. "How nice."

Lady Speely's cheeks turned pink and she darted Aislin a nasty glance, as if the princess had done something terrible.

Prince Rory finished helping himself from a platter and turned to Aislin. "It's the strangest thing, but I feel as if I've seen you somewhere before."

"In the hall, yesterday," Tomas told him.

"I don't recall seeing ... Oh, the servant girl!" Rory said. "That was you?"

Aislin blushed bright red. He had been talking about *her* when he told the others about Tomas's interaction with a plump servant girl? She had never thought of herself as plump. Although she wasn't as thin as her fairy relatives, she was no heavier than her mother or the other pedrasi, and none of them were considered plump! They were all nicely rounded and well-proportioned; everyone thought they looked just the way they should.

"Will you ever learn to keep your mouth shut?" Tomas asked the prince.

Rory shrugged and turned to talk to his father.

Aislin stared down at her trencher. Suddenly Lady Speely's comments took on new meaning. She hadn't been trying to help; she had been deliberately hurtful on the queen's behalf! It hadn't been lack of skill or taste that had made the gowns so awful.

Aislin's face flamed a second time as she thought about how naive she had been. These weren't the good-hearted fey who loved her and her family. These were humans who seemed to take pleasure in hurting the feelings of others. Well, it wasn't going to happen again; she'd make sure of that! Sitting up straight in her seat,

Aislin glanced at Lady Speely. The woman had better stay away from her. Aislin had dealt with much worse creatures than a rude human woman.

As angry as Aislin felt, she didn't dare open her mouth. Not only did she not want these women to know that they had gotten to her, she also didn't want any of them guessing that she wasn't exactly what they thought she was—a human like themselves. Making the stone floor shake now would be a very bad idea.

"You really should try the pickled beets," Tomas told her as another server came by. When Aislin looked at him, he added, "I noticed you didn't help yourself to any meat, so I thought the beets might appeal to you."

Tomas really was different, Aislin decided. Seeing the kindness in his eyes went a long way to ease her anger. He was the only human who'd been consistently nice to her, and she couldn't help but like him. Taking a deep breath to calm herself, she gave him a grateful smile. "I think I will, thank you," she said, and helped herself from the platter. As the server walked away, she turned back to Tomas. "You said that you've been here a few months. Where do you come from originally?"

"Scarmander," he said.

"Ah, the kingdom to the south," Aislin replied, remembering what she'd seen from the clouds.

"Southwest of Morain, really," Tomas told her.

"And why are you here?" she asked.

"I'm here for my own good," Tomas said, lowering his voice. "Or at least that's what King Tyburr says."

"I see," said Aislin, glancing at the king, but he and the prince were deep in conversation about Rory's schooling and hadn't heard Tomas. Perhaps she wasn't the only one unhappy to be in Morain. She'd have to have a private conversation with Tomas as soon as she could manage it.

They talked then about inconsequential things like the food, the banners, and the shields draping the walls of the Great Hall, and the way some people ate with no manners at all. Tomas had her laughing until her sides hurt as he pointed out particular offenders among the people they could see from the dais.

When supper was nearly over and the sugared cakes had been served, a minstrel carrying a lute took the floor. He sang a song that was pleasant enough, but every time he hit a wrong note it hurt Aislin's sensitive hearing, inherited from her father's side, and she winced. Aislin didn't think anyone else minded, but after a round of polite applause, he was about to start a second song and King Tyburr waved him away. "I used to think that Grady's singing was very good, until I heard a voice that was glorious. Princess Aislin, would you be so kind as to sing for us?"

Aislin hadn't been expecting this, but she didn't know how to get out of it. Everyone was looking at her expectantly, including Tomas. Clearing her throat, Aislin got to her feet and looked around the room. She couldn't sing to them while thinking that they were all like the queen and her family, but if she thought of them as people like Tomas, she could do her very best.

Closing her eyes, Aislin began a song about love and loss and finding love again. The song was originally about fairies and their loves over the many long years, but she changed it so it was about humans whose love returned when they were getting old. When she opened her eyes, half the people were crying. The rest were trying hard not to cry. She started a pedrasi drinking song next, one that was so old that the ancestors of the people in the room might have heard it. Aislin was only halfway through the song when a messenger hurried in and ran to the king's side. After a whispered conversation, the king got up and left the hall. Aislin kept singing, but she noticed that the queen looked anxious and fidgeted until the song was over.

People were still clapping when the queen stood

and left the hall. "Nice singing," the prince told Aislin, then he, too, walked out.

People all around the room started to stand. A group of young ladies hurried to join Princess Selene, pointing at Aislin and laughing. Aislin stood when she noticed that Lady Speely was looking her way. Talking to Lady Speely would be a terrible idea right now; she doubted very much that she'd be able to control her temper. Turning to Tomas, Aislin said, "Would you mind walking me to my corridor? I'm not sure I remember the way."

"I'd be happy to," he said, standing up to lead her off the dais. "Rory is a rude idiot, but he was right about one thing—you do look lovely in that gown."

"Thank you, but I know you're only saying that to be nice," said Aislin.

Tomas shook his head. "No, it's the truth. I never lie, ever."

Aislin glanced at him in amazement. If it was true, Tomas was the first person she had ever met who could honestly make that claim. The very thought was refreshing.

Instead of heading for the stairs, Aislin turned the other way so they were standing in the empty end of the corridor. "Before we say good night, I'd like to ask you something," she told him. "What you said about King Tyburr bringing you here for your own good—was it against your will?"

Tomas nodded. "It was. I was just inside the border when his men found me. He refuses to let me leave."

"He brought me here because he thought he was saving me from a terrible home, but I don't think he ever told us the real reason he had gone to my parents' kingdom," said Aislin. "Something is going on; I just don't know what it might be. I would love to go home soon, though I'm not sure how to arrange it."

"King Tyburr wouldn't have brought you here if it hadn't suited him for some reason. He probably wants something from your kingdom. That may explain your very informal welcome to the castle. Normally a king would have a welcoming ceremony for a visiting princess and treat her with far more respect, but he may be trying to downplay your presence here so no one suspects what he has in mind. The herald said you were from Eliasind. I've never heard of it," said Tomas.

"You wouldn't have," Aislin told him. "It's secluded and not very well known. Why do you suppose King Tyburr wants you here?"

"Because he hopes to control my father through me," said Tomas. "My father is the Duke of Isely, the most powerful man in Scarmander. He's also heir to Ozwalt, King of Scarmander. Morain and Scarmander have fought off and on for most of our history. We had peace for a time, but we've been on the brink of starting another war for the last year. Both kingdoms claim possession of an island in the middle of the Galiman River that forms part of the border between us. The best walnut trees found anywhere in the world grow on the island, and the fishing around the island is phenomenal. When fighting broke out between the fishermen of our two kingdoms, both sides sent soldiers to maintain the peace. If there was to be a war, my father would lead the Scarmander army. I was on a mission for my father that would have kept this war from happening, but then King Tyburr's men found me. King Tyburr brought me here so he could question me about Father. Now I think the king believes that my father won't fight as long as I'm in Morain, which is why he refuses to let me go. I see signs that the king is gearing up for war every day. Have you noticed how many soldiers are here now? There weren't nearly as many when I first arrived."

Aislin nodded, thinking about everything she had just learned. "I wondered why there were so many. I need to find out why King Tyburr might want me here; my parents' kingdom has no role in your wars."

She sighed and glanced down the corridor. "I suppose I should go upstairs now. I have some thinking to do." *And some spies to send out,* she thought. *Poppy likes her excursions and Twinket is finally going to get her very own errand.*

Chapter 10

NEITHER POPPY NOR TWINKET was back from her investigation when Aislin fell asleep that night. She dreamed that she was home in Eliasind, swimming in Blue Lake with Poppy, Bim, and some of their water nymph friends. Twinket was there as well, watching over them from the shore. They were splashing and playing when suddenly something rose from the depths of the lake. It had a horrible face and long, hairy arms that ended in two grasping claws. Terrible things spewed from its mouth, and the creature grew as it swam closer until it threatened to fill the entire lake.

"It's a human!" Bim cried as they all tried to get away.

Aislin jolted awake just as the sun was coming up. Twinket was sitting in the chair by the window, looking out at the clouds. The doll turned when she heard Aislin stir, and jumped up when she saw that the princess had opened her eyes.

"Finally!" cried the doll. "Do you know how long I've been waiting to talk to you? I have so much to tell you!"

"Shouldn't we wait for Poppy?" said Aislin. "I want you both here for your reports."

"I'll get her!" Twinket said, and ran into the dressing room.

"I didn't mean that you should wake her!" Aislin called after her.

"I don't mind," Poppy said, rubbing her eyes as she came into the room. "I was just dozing."

The fairy sat on the floor cross-legged, yawning so widely that Aislin could see all her teeth.

"How did it go?" Aislin asked her friends. She noticed how the morning sunlight glinted on Poppy's hair and was suddenly suspicious. "Did you do more magic in this room?"

Poppy looked away, no longer able to meet her eyes. "Maybe a little," she said. "You were tossing and turning in your sleep when I came back, so I used a sleep-well spell on you."

127

"I said no more magic!" Aislin began.

"May I please give my report?" said Twinket. "I have so much to tell you!"

Aislin sighed. "Go ahead," she told her little friend, although her eyes flicked a warning at the fairy.

"I went to Prince Rory's room, and it was just where you told me it was," Twinket told Poppy. "He was in there talking to a man who was helping him get ready for bed. Why would anyone need help getting ready for bed?"

"Because they're ill?" said Poppy. "Or just plain lazy."

"Go on," said Aislin.

"Anyway, Prince Rory talked the whole time. I think he likes to hear his own voice, because he even talked when I was sure the man wasn't listening. I know *I* didn't want to hear what he was saying because he was just plain rude. He told the man he was incompetent, and demanded he wash a certain shirt, then he started talking about Aislin. That's when I really started to hate him."

"What did he say?" Aislin asked. "Tell it to me just like he said it, if you can. I want to hear it all."

"Are you sure? It wasn't very nice," said Twinket.

128

Aislin nodded. "I'm sure. I need to hear the truth, so don't change it just so it sounds better."

"All right. If that's what you want," replied Twinket. "He said that his father says that he should think about marrying you, but that's never going to happen. He said that he refuses to have a plump wife when there are so many thin girls around. He said that he'd never even heard of the kingdom you came from, so it must not be important. Then he got quiet for a minute. I don't know if he was thinking or the man was pulling a sleep shirt over his head. I couldn't see them very well. Then he said that your face is beautiful, and that you have the prettiest eyes he'd ever seen. He said if you lost some weight he might consider it. He said maybe he should tell you that and then you would do it because he's such a good catch. And then the man left the room and Rory stopped talking."

"What he said was quite enough," Aislin said through tight lips. "A great catch! If I were fishing for my supper and he was the only fish in the lake, I'd throw him back and starve!"

"Wait, there's more!" Twinket declared. "I was really mad when he said those things about you, so I waited until he was asleep and snoring really loudly.

I opened his door just enough that I could squeeze in, then I collected all his shoes and stuffed them in a fancy-looking bag. I hauled them back into the secret space behind the wall and dragged them to a dark corner far away where no one will ever find them. That's what took me so long."

Poppy laughed. "You should have come to get me. I would have sent them to the dung heap and buried them like that!" She snapped her fingers. Fairy dust sparkled at her fingertips, giving a warm glow to the room. "I might even have sent *him* along with the shoes."

"Poppy!" Aislin warned. "Your fingers dust like that only when you're thinking about using magic."

"I'm sorry, but I hate this 'no magic' thing," said Poppy. "Back home, magic is as natural as breathing!"

"I know," said Aislin. "But we're not home now and we have to be careful."

Poppy was still making a scowly face when Twinket said, "Now it's your turn. What did you find out?"

"I went to the king's bedchamber first, but he wasn't there," said Poppy. "So I went to his secret room behind the secret door and there he was, talking to a bunch of men. They were looking at a map, but I couldn't see more than a little corner of it. They said a whole lot that I didn't understand about some war starting, and then they said something that I thought was really important. The whole reason the king went to Eliasind is because he's looking for a back way into a place called Salamander."

"Scarmander," Aislin corrected. "That's probably why he asked me if I'd ever visited the southern mountains. He wanted to find out if I knew of a way through."

"He said that he didn't find it the first time he looked, but he's going to go back, and he's going to take you," said Poppy.

"He's taking me home!" Aislin said, suddenly excited.

Poppy squinched her eyes and shook her head. "Not really. At least not in a good way. He said that he brought you here because you'd saved his life and he thought he owed it to you to take you away from 'the monsters in the castle.' But he said that he's been giving it a lot of thought and he thinks you can be useful. He plans to take you back to Eliasind as his hostage. He'll threaten to hurt you if your family doesn't cooperate and show him how to get his army into Salaman... Scarmander."

Aislin went cold all over. At what point had she gone from being a rescued guest to a hostage he could threaten? She'd thought that the king was capable of lying after he was so secretive about his trip to Eliasind, but she didn't think he'd go this far! There was no way she would let him use her against her family like that!

She thought furiously, trying to come up with a way to dissuade him, until it occurred to her that if he couldn't get through the pass, he wouldn't have the chance to do anything so awful.

"I need to get word to my parents to make sure no one can use the pass again," Aislin told her friends. "They have to make it super secure and they need to do it now."

"I could go tell them," said Poppy. "But it would take me a few days to fly there and I wouldn't be able to get in if the pass is already closed."

"If you were gone that long, someone would be sure to notice that you were missing," Aislin told her. "No, I think we'll have to send a message with a bird. If the pass is closed and the bird can't get in, then the message isn't necessary. But if it can get in, it would be a lot faster."

"I don't know if I can call one from here," Poppy said, glancing at the window.

"Let me see," said Aislin as she got to her feet. She went to the window, but didn't see any birds. None of the pigeons, sparrows, doves, or crows that normally lived around castles were anywhere in sight.

Poppy and Twinket joined her at the window. "I don't see a single bird," said Twinket. "Maybe there are too many cats here."

"I'll see what I can do," Poppy told her friends and made a summoning whistle. After waiting a short time, she tried again, but they still didn't see any birds.

"They aren't coming," said Twinket. "Try one more time and make it louder."

Poppy stuck her head out the window and called once more. She was backing away from the window when a whoosh of large wings heralded a falcon dropping from the sky. The bird landed on the windowsill, and looked up at the fairy.

Aislin covered her ears at the bird's loud shriek, but Poppy listened intently. The fairy replied, then the bird responded. Aislin waited while they spoke, wishing once more that translating wasn't necessary.

Finally, Poppy turned to Aislin. "He didn't want to do it until I promised him that your family would reward him. What do you want him to tell them?"

"Tell him that if all the passes are closed, he won't be able to deliver my message," said Aislin. "But if even one is open the tiniest bit, he has to go through the pass and tell any bird he meets that this message is for the royal family of Eliasind. The bird should help him find his way to the castle. When he gets there, he needs to give the royal family this message: *Princess Aislin is in good health. King Tyburr of Morain is going to war with Scarmander. He wants to sneak into that kingdom through Eliasind. He plans to use Aislin as a hostage to force you to help him. Make sure the passes are closed. Don't worry about Aislin. She can take care of herself.*"

Poppy repeated Aislin's words to the falcon. When the bird held up his leg to show her the long jesses tied to it, she pointed her finger at him. Golden sparkles glittered in the sunlight as the leather strips fell away.

The falcon cried out, hopped from the ledge, and circled the tower across from the window. When they couldn't see him anymore, Poppy turned to Aislin and asked, "Do you think he'll do it? We don't know that bird at all."

"He will if he wants that reward," said Aislin.

"Do you want to go for a walk?" Poppy asked her. "I've never seen the garden in daylight."

"I'd love to," Aislin told her. "I'll be ready in a minute."

Aislin had just finished changing her clothes when there was a knock on the door. Before anyone could answer, Lady Speely walked in. Thankfully, she didn't notice Twinket go limp and fall over. "You owe me an explanation," she told Aislin. "Where did you get the gown you wore last night?"

All the anger Aislin had felt in the Great Hall the night before came back in a rush, but she knew that if she said anything right then, the entire castle might shake. Using every bit of control that she could muster, she did her best not to let any of the power in her affect the stone. "Lady Speely," she said, nearly choking on the name. "You will address me as Your Highness. My father is a king and I am *Princess* Aislin."

Lady Speely looked away, no longer able to meet her gaze. Holding her head high, Aislin continued. "I don't owe you anything. You, however, owe me an apology. I know that you were trying to humiliate me with that horrid gown and you are angry because it didn't work, and now Queen Tatya is unhappy with you. That's your problem, not mine. Get out of my room and don't ever come here again. I don't want to have anything more to do with you. Poppy, please see this awful woman out."

Lady Speely's mouth opened and closed, but she

didn't seem able to speak. Although she no longer looked directly at Aislin, the princess noticed that the woman's eyes glistened with tears. "I ... I'm sorry," she finally choked out as Poppy took her by the arm and pushed her out the door.

"Stay away from Princess Aislin, or you'll have to deal with me!" Poppy declared, and slammed the door behind her.

The girls waited until they heard Lady Speely's footsteps retreat down the hall. "Did you see that?" Poppy asked her friends. "She was actually starting to cry. I didn't think that heartless beast was capable of it. I think you managed to make her feel bad, Aislin. You must have put power in your voice and it worked on a human!"

"That's not surprising if you think about it," said Twinket. "Anyone who can control stone with her voice like Aislin shouldn't find it hard to influence a human's emotions. Although I think Lady Speely deserves to be punished more than that. I can think of lots of things we can do to her! I could—"

"We're not doing anything unless she continues to bother me," said Aislin. "Twinket, Poppy and I won't be gone long. Stay here and don't do anything to anyone!"

Walking through the castle was a lot more fun for Aislin when Poppy was with her. They pointed out interesting things to each other and both laughed when they saw the prince wearing shoes that obviously didn't fit. Poppy whispered, "There's one!" when they passed a secret door. A few minutes later, Aislin saw one that Poppy had missed. It seemed that the humans had lots of secrets.

Aislin was pleased that the garden was empty when they arrived, but she doubted it would stay that way for long. The two girls strolled to the far end where the lily pond formed a perfect circle. Aislin sat on the stone edge of the pond and leaned toward the water. There was no wind today, and the water was still. She had dipped her hand in the pool and was swirling it around when a small yellow feather drifted down onto the water's surface. Aislin looked up. A flock of goldfinches was fluttering around Poppy, chirping madly.

Once again, Poppy had to translate. "They say that they came as soon as they could. They heard me call, but they couldn't come before this because they were afraid of the falcon that some nasty man lets out at the same time every day. They said that they saw the falcon fly away, and the man didn't let any more birds out, so they knew they could answer my call. They want to know why I summoned them."

"Please thank them for coming, but tell them that we've already handled our problem," Aislin told her.

As Poppy was talking to the finches, Aislin heard voices just beyond the hedge.

"Poppy, someone is coming," said Aislin. "It would look odd if you're found talking to a flock of goldfinches."

Poppy chirped something to the little birds, who flew off in a swirl of yellow, darting across the garden and over the castle wall. "I've always liked goldfinches," Poppy told Aislin. "They're such cheerful birds! Oh, wait. I hear the voices now, too."

"One sounds like Princess Selene," said Aislin. "I really don't want to talk to her."

"I could look for a back way out, but I think it's too late," Poppy replied.

Aislin sighed. "Never mind. I'll have to talk to her sometime. It might as well be now."

Princess Selene and a group of girls her age appeared at the entrance to the garden. When they saw Aislin, Selene waved and called, "There you are! We were hoping we'd find you."

Aislin wished she was anyplace else but here, even as she returned her wave. "I'll see you back at the room," Poppy said, stepping aside as Selene hurried over, wearing a friendly smile.

"I'd like to invite you to my chambers for an impromptu concert," Selene said to Aislin. "We all loved your singing and want to hear more. Would you join us? We have my room all set up for it."

"I suppose," Aislin replied, not sure how to get out of it without being rude.

"We really should get to know one another better," Selene said, hooking her arm through Aislin's. "I understand that you might be my sister-in-law someday."

Not a chance! thought Aislin, though she gave in to the pressure on her arm and started to walk with Selene.

Aislin wondered what she could possibly have to say to the human princess, but she didn't have to worry. The group of girls that clustered around them kept up a lively conversation all the way to Selene's rooms, leaving no time for anyone else to say anything. The three girls named Merrilee, Joselle, and Laneece did most of the talking.

When they opened the door, Aislin saw that Selene had a suite of rooms that were much larger than the one she'd been given. They had entered a huge sitting room with three other doors leading off to one side. The furniture was fancier than and not nearly as dark as Aislin had seen elsewhere in the castle. A portrait over the fireplace showed a young woman with golden curls and a saucy smile. Her eyes were vivid green and the tip of her nose was tilted.

"What a pretty girl!" Aislin exclaimed.

"You think she's pretty?" Joselle scoffed. "I think her nose is odd. It certainly isn't perfect like a real princess's."

"You can't tell it from the portrait, but they say she was as plump as a partridge," said Merrilee.

"Queen Tatya says she was a silly goose," added Laneece.

Selene's voice sounded odd when she said, "You told me that you had everything ready for Aislin to sing for us. Let's begin."

The three girls hurried to a curtain that hung from ceiling to floor, dividing the front of the room from the back. A row of chairs had been set up facing the curtain, and the girls directed Selene to the chair in the middle.

"Good! Now you come with us," Merrilee told Aislin, leading her behind the curtain. "Wait on this side until we're ready. We'll be just a minute."

Aislin looked around while the girls fumbled with the curtain on the other side. All the furniture that normally filled the room had been shoved up against the wall, leaving her very little space to stand. She turned to face the curtain, waiting while the other girls took their seats. When it was finally quiet, Laneece called out, "We're ready. You may begin."

Aislin reached for the curtain, trying to find a way to open it. She felt her way across, but it seemed to be one solid piece. The girls must have fastened the two halves together. "I can't find my way out of here," she called out as she continued to look.

Merrilee laughed. "You silly goose! You have to stand on that side. We want to hear your singing; we don't want to look at you! Your voice is lovely, but seeing you would be too distracting."

The girls laughed, a shrill sound that grated on Aislin's ears. The hand that was gripping the fabric turned into a fist.

"Did you know that you'd be quite beautiful if only you lost some weight?" called Laneece.

The girls laughed again until Joselle called out, "And covered up those strange eyes. No one has eyes that color or pupils so big."

Aislin's hand shook, making the curtain shake

with it. No one had ever spoken to her like this. These girls were being deliberately nasty, if only to amuse each other.

"You shouldn't spend so much time in the sun. A princess shouldn't have tanned skin," cried Merrilee.

Aislin had had more than enough. No one should be so disrespectful to a princess! Especially not one who was both fairy and pedrasi royalty! She had never thought of herself as superior to anyone before, but she was certainly better than these horrible girls. Unable to find a way through the curtain, Aislin took another way out. Drawing power from the floor, she pulled the curtain down so hard that the whole thing fell to the floor, taking part of the ceiling with it.

The girls screamed and jumped to their feet, even though they were all too far from the curtain to have been hurt. Aislin was disgusted. They were nasty and cowards and didn't deserve her respect.

"You should be ashamed of yourselves, talking to anyone that way!" Aislin said, putting power into her words. With her head held high, she stalked from the room, barely noticing the horrified look Selene was giving her friends.

Aislin was on her way to her own room when a voice called out to her. "Is everything all right?"

She would have kept going, but she recognized Tomas's voice. "No, it's not all right!" she snapped. But when she saw the hurt look on Tomas's face, she suddenly felt contrite.

"I didn't mean—" Tomas began.

"No, I'm sorry," said Aislin. "It's not your fault. I'm in a bad mood because of something Selene's friends just did. Those girls are absolutely the worst people I have ever met."

"I know," said Tomas. "I discovered that my first day here. If it's any consolation, I told them so to their faces once."

Aislin laughed. "I'm glad. Now I can think of all sorts of things I should have said, but I was in too much of a hurry to leave."

"Isn't that always the way it goes!" Tomas said with a grin.

"I've been meaning to ask you about that book you were reading," said Aislin. "Did you get to finish it?"

Tomas shook his head. "No, I didn't, although I wanted to. I was close to the end when Rory grabbed it out of my hand and said that he wanted to read it. When I said I wasn't finished with it, he threatened to tear the book up, so I let him have it. I didn't know he could read."

"He probably can't," Aislin told him. "My ... servant ... found the book in the trash. I can give it to you at supper tonight if you'd like."

"That would be great! Thanks! It's good to know that there are some nice people in this kingdom and not everyone is like Rory or those girls." Tomas gave her the warmest smile she'd seen all day.

Chapter 11

AISLIN WAS ON HER way to supper with the book in her pocket when a stir ran through the crowd in the corridor. She kept wondering what was going on—until a woman with gray hair stopped to tell another woman walking in front of Aislin, "I just learned that the queen has been in labor since last night!"

Aislin looked around, smiling. At home this would have been a good reason to celebrate.

"I hope everything goes all right," said the second woman.

"I hope it's a boy, for the king's sake," a woman said as she came down the steps. "He so wants another son."

"I hope it doesn't interfere with my supper," said the man at her side. "Prince Rory was born just as we sat down to eat. The king was so excited that he forgot to tell us we could begin. No one knew what to do, so we waited until he came back. By then our supper was cold."

"Something is going wrong with the birth," another woman said as a larger crowd began to gather. "I heard it from a page who just came from the queen's rooms."

Aislin pushed through the chattering people, very few of whom seemed to care much about the queen or the new baby at all. In Eliasind, the good health of the mother and child would have been the primary concern; listening to the gossip around her, Aislin's dislike for the people in King Tyburr's court only deepened.

Her whole life, her parents had taught her that people had to help each other; the more power you had, the more you needed to give. King Carrigan used magic and diplomacy to help others. Queen Maylin used her ability to heal.

When Maylin was a girl, she'd fixed a deer's broken leg and discovered her healing skills. After that, she'd spent years trying to figure out how to handle her ability. Aislin had been eight when the queen discovered that her daughter had the same talent for healing and began to teach her at every opportunity.

Although Aislin was still young, she had attended dozens of births, helping her mother and learning what needed to be done. If Queen Tatya's labor was in difficulty, Aislin had to try to help. She may not like the queen, but denying her help went against everything she'd been taught.

For just the briefest moment, Aislin thought about asking for directions, but she knew right away that no one was going to tell her where the queen's rooms were located. Instead, she walked away from the crowd and pressed her hand against the stone wall. The castle itself could tell her where she needed to go.

With her mind linked to the stone, Aislin hurried down the corridor and up the stairs. Another corridor and three turns brought her to the door leading to Queen Tatya's rooms. Women were scurrying in and out, fetching water and bringing news. The men waiting outside the room barely spared Aislin a glance as she hurried in after one of the women. The first room she entered was an antechamber where women clustered around, talking in low voices. The next room was the bedchamber where Queen Tatya lay, barely moving. Most of the women in this room looked lost and frightened, as if they had no idea what to do. They were clustered around the only woman who seemed to have any idea what was going on, hanging on her every word.

"The baby's stuck," she said. "It's not coming out the way it should. The poor queen has been in hard labor for far too long and is exhausted. I don't know if either of them will make it."

Aislin pushed past the women to the queen's bedside. Tatya's eyes were closed as she turned her head to the side, moaning. She was drenched in perspiration and her face was waxy pale.

"You there! What are you doing?" asked the woman who seemed to be in charge.

"What you appear to be unable to do. I've come to help the queen," Aislin told her.

"How dare you!" the woman exclaimed. "I'm the Royal Midwife, and if I can't help her, no one can."

Aislin sighed, knowing she didn't have time to deal with the women. Recalling how she'd stood up to Lady Speely and later to Princess Selene's friends, she drew strength from the stone floor and put it into her voice. "You will stay out of my way while I help the queen," she said. "When I am gone, you will forget that I was here."

She wasn't sure if her commands would work or not, but the women did turn away and leave her alone.

Placing her hand on the queen's forehead, Aislin said, "I'm here. I'll help you now. Everything is going to be all right."

The queen's eyes fluttered open for a moment, then closed as another contraction gripped her body. Aislin placed her other hand on the queen's belly and closed her own eyes. Reaching with her mind into the stone floor, she drew up the strength she needed, using it to ease the queen's pain and shift the baby in her womb the smallest amount. When Aislin opened her eyes again, color was coming back into the queen's cheeks and the midwife was crying, "The baby is coming!"

Satisfied that she'd done what was needed, Aislin stepped back and slipped from the room unnoticed. If all went well, no one would remember that she'd been there. Talk about how she'd helped the queen would only draw more attention to her, which was the last thing she wanted.

Suddenly hungry, Aislin hurried to the Great Hall and was pleased to see that Tomas was already there. He was the only one at the table.

"Aren't Rory and Selene coming?" Aislin asked as she took her seat.

"I don't know," said Tomas. "I haven't talked to

either of them all day. They both seem to be agitated about one thing or another. Did you bring the book?"

"I did," Aislin said, taking it out of her pocket. "I'm afraid it has a torn page."

Tomas examined the book and nodded. "Rory did that when he took it from me. At least he didn't rip it out."

They started talking about the book, not really noticing as the food was brought out with little order or ceremony. The people at the lower tables talked louder than usual, but Aislin and Tomas enjoyed their supper as if they were far removed from everyone. When Aislin realized that no one could possibly hear them, she leaned closer to Tomas and said, "You mentioned a mission for your father that would prevent the war from happening. What were you supposed to do?"

"Give something to someone," said Tomas. "That's all I can say. Please don't ask any more questions about it, because I really shouldn't even have told you that much."

"I won't," promised Aislin. "At least not until you're ready to tell me."

They had almost finished eating when a page rushed into the room to announce, "The queen has had a girl! There's a new royal princess! Both Queen Tatya and the infant are doing well."

People shouted for more wine to celebrate. As the crowd grew rowdier, Aislin decided that it was time for her to leave.

"I'll walk you upstairs," said Tomas, then added in a quieter voice, "There's something that I think I should tell you."

Aislin nodded and got to her feet. He had sounded serious enough to make her start to worry; she had a feeling that she wasn't going to like whatever he had to say. They didn't talk again until they reached Aislin's room. Poppy looked surprised to see Tomas. Although the fairy disappeared into the dressing room, Twinket stayed sprawled on the floor by the window.

"I hear things now and then," Tomas began. "I'm big and people often think I'm not too bright because I tell the truth even when a lie would be more helpful. A lot of them aren't careful about what they say when they're around me. Last night Rory was saying that his father was taking a trip soon and you were going with him. He didn't say where or why, but I thought you should know."

"The king has barely spoken to me since I got here. He certainly hasn't said anything to me about a trip, but I think I already know where and why," said Aislin.

"He's probably planning to spring it on you at the last minute," Tomas told her. "He does that a lot."

"Thank you for the warning," Aislin said. "I don't like that kind of surprise."

Tomas shrugged. "Neither of us wants to be here, and I have a feeling that we're both being used. I think we should help each other whenever we can."

The moment the door closed behind Tomas, Twinket sat up and Poppy came back in the room. "Did you hear that?" Aislin asked her friends.

"I sure did," said Twinket. "I think that boy likes you."

"I heard it, too," Poppy declared. "It sounds as if King Tyburr is getting ready to go back to Eliasind soon."

There was a knock on the door. Aislin glanced from Poppy to Twinket. Could the king be ready to go now?

While Twinket went limp, Poppy answered the door. It was a footman, who bowed when he saw the princess. "Her Highness, Princess Selene, requests the honor of your presence as soon as possible," he said.

"Thank you," Aislin replied, and nodded for Poppy to close the door.

"At least it wasn't a summons from the king," said Twinket as she got to her feet.

"No, but this is almost as bad," Aislin told her friends. "I'd really rather not see Selene again."

"Why? What happened?" asked Poppy. "You didn't tell us about your visit to her rooms."

"I know," said Aislin. "I didn't want to talk about it because it made me so angry. Her friends said some horrible things to me and thought they were being funny. I got mad and tore down a curtain and left in a huff. I knew it was wrong as soon as I stormed out of the room. No normal human could have pulled down that curtain like that, and I know I shouldn't act any way but human. I'm not sorry I lost my temper, though. I stood up for myself when those girls were being terribly rude.

"I did something else, too. I put power in my voice, like I did when Lady Speely came to rant at me after we fixed the dresses. It's funny, though…it's been a long time since I learned how to pull power from stone, to tell it what to do, but I've never used the power on anything but the stone itself before. Certainly not on a person. When I spoke to Lady Speely, I was trying not to make the stone shake—I guess I ended up using the power on her instead. I was as surprised as you were when I made her cry. After Selene's friends were so horrible, I told them that they should be ashamed of themselves. When I left, some of them looked as if they might be. Just now in the queen's room, I used power in my voice on her ladies to make sure they wouldn't interfere when I tried to help. I also told them not to remember me. I hope it worked."

"You helped the queen, after the way she treated you?" said Poppy. "That was awfully good of you."

Aislin shrugged. "I heard that she was in distress, so I went to her."

"Well, I think you did the right thing when you told those girls off!" said Twinket. "I would have given them all a good kick in the seat, too! Maybe you shouldn't go see Selene. Who knows what she has planned?"

"I would be foolish to go see her and fall for the same thing twice," Aislin admitted.

Poppy shook her head. "I can't believe she would do that again. What if she wants to see you about something else entirely?"

Aislin sighed. "I know. If I don't go, I'll wonder if I really should have. All right—I'm going. But there's something I need you to do, Poppy. I want you to play spy again and find out what's going on. Go back to the king's hidden room and see what he's planning. Don't let anyone see you and don't use any magic. I need to know what King Tyburr is thinking so I can be prepared for whatever he has in mind."

"And I can check on Rory," Twinket declared. "He's always interesting."

Aislin was still wondering if she'd made the wrong decision, even as she knocked on the door to Selene's rooms. Instead of a maid, the princess opened it herself; she seemed to be alone. "Thank you for coming," Selene said as she ushered Aislin into the room. "I wasn't sure you would after what happened when you were here before."

"I almost didn't," Aislin admitted. She noticed that the curtain was gone, the ceiling was patched, and the furniture was in position again.

"I'm glad you came," Selene told her as she gestured to a chair. The girls sat across from each other on either side of the fireplace. When Aislin was settled, Selene glanced up at the portrait. "That young woman was my mother. I felt so ashamed after what my so-called friends said to you. I didn't stand up for you or for my mother, and I feel horrible about it."

"They aren't your friends?" asked Aislin.

Selene shook her head. "Not really. They're the daughters of some of Queen Tatya's ladies. I never knew any of them until Tatya married my father. She made me take them on as my ladies-in-waiting. I've tried to treat them like my friends because I wanted to make Tatya happy, but they aren't very nice and I'm tired of overlooking their pettiness and the unkind things they say. It's time I stood up to them and demand that they treat people with more respect—including my mother, even though she's no longer here."

Aislin glanced up at the portrait again. Seeing the young woman's smiling face made her miss her own mother. Although Aislin loved everyone in her family very much, had she been guilty of not giving the pedrasi side the same respect that she gave the fairies? After all, Aislin had convinced herself that fairies, with their showy magic, were better than the pedrasi, whose abilities with stone rarely drew attention. But even now, living among humans, she was learning how much she didn't know about what her mother's people could do.

"Why were they saying such awful things about your mother?" asked Aislin. "Even they should have known that was too much."

"Probably because they've overheard Tatya saying those things. My parents were madly in love with each other; everyone knew it. After my mother died, my father didn't remarry for a while. Then his advisors started telling him he should, right around the time he met Tatya on a state visit. He liked her well enough at first, but he didn't love her, not the way he did my mother. Even before she came here, Tatya resented my mother. I think she says mean things about her so people won't remember my mother as such a good person … but it's really just making them not like Tatya. I have to tell you something else, too—it's been obvious that Lady Speely hasn't liked you since you first arrived. That horrible woman came here with Tatya and always sides with her. She's Tatya's spy and confidant, and I know she hates my mother just as much as the queen does. I think you remind them both of my mother somehow, which is maybe why they have been so awful to you. I just wanted you to know that it really doesn't have anything to do with you personally."

"Thank you for telling me," said Aislin. It didn't make up for the women's pettiness, but she was grateful to learn why they behaved the way they did.

"And thank you for saying that my mother was pretty. I always thought she was, too."

"But she *was* pretty," Aislin said, gazing up at the portrait. *And Selene is beautiful,* she thought, looking at the girl across from her. *I wonder why she doesn't look anything like either of her parents.*

"Tatya never met her," said Selene. "I don't think she would say such things about her if she had. After you left, I sent the girls away and I looked for this letter." Reaching to a small table beside her chair, she picked up a folded piece of parchment. "My mother wrote this to me when she was dying. She was a good, kind person. She wanted me to believe in myself and be kind, too. I forgot all that while I was trying to please Tatya, but it's time I remembered what my mother tried to teach me. I don't think those girls will change, so I think it's time I made new friends. I was hoping that you would be one of them."

"I'd like that," Aislin told her.

The two princesses talked for a while about the castle and the people in it. When Aislin finally left, she was feeling better about what had happened the last time she'd visited the princess's rooms. If a little shame had opened Selene's eyes, maybe it had all been worth it.

When Aislin returned to her chamber, neither Poppy nor Twinket was there. She sat up, waiting for her friends to return, and was relieved when Twinket slipped into the room.

"The more I know about that boy Rory, the more I can't stand him," Twinket said as she settled on the floor at Aislin's feet. "He's happy because the new baby isn't a boy. He thinks that the king might like another boy better than him and make the new one his heir. Apparently, a girl can't inherit the crown in Morain."

"Really?" said Aislin. "How odd. Did Rory say anything else?"

Twinket giggled. "He mostly talked about finding the thief who took his shoes. I think I should take something else now. Or maybe I'll draw a picture of him on his mirror and give him a big nose and ginormous ears!"

"You will do no such thing!" Aislin scolded her. "No more tricks or taking things. I don't want people looking around for the culprit and finding you."

"It was just an idea," the doll grumbled.

"Ideas are fine. Just don't actually *do* any of them," said Aislin.

"Okay!" Twinket replied. "Want to hear some of my other ideas?"

They came up with one idea after another for things they could do to Rory, if only they weren't trying to keep their real identities secret. They were still laughing at each other's suggestions when Poppy returned to the room.

Seeing the serious look on her fairy friend's face, Aislin no longer felt like laughing. "What did you find out?" she asked.

"I'm sorry it took so long, but the king was alone in the room for a while; he didn't say anything until that man Craiger showed up," said Poppy. "King Tyburr is disappointed that the baby is a girl. He really wanted another son."

"What is wrong with these people?" said Aislin. "All the fey know that girls are just as good as boys."

"Even better sometimes," Twinket chimed in.

"Humans are crazy, that's all there is to it," said Poppy. "Oh, and King Tyburr is mad that he has to stay here until after the christening and postpone his plans to go back to Eliasind. The christening is going to be held the day after tomorrow, which is the soonest they can have it arranged."

"Good. That will give the falcon more time to

160

reach the land between the mountains and get the message to my parents. Thank you for your help." Aislin turned from one friend to the other. "I don't know what I'd have done if I'd come here by myself."

"Missed me, that's for sure!" said Twinket.

Chapter 12

AISLIN STAYED IN HER room the next day, sending
Poppy out to get their meals and news of what was
happening in the castle. Aside from the frenzied prep-
arations for the christening, there wasn't much else
for her to report. Selene was having a new gown made,
Rory was still hunting for the shoe thief, and King
Tyburr was talking to Craiger and his commanders
about warlike things that Poppy didn't understand.

The christening was held midmorning two days
after the baby was born. Everyone entered the Great
Hall dressed in their finest clothes to honor the baby
princess. Even the servants had been invited. Poppy
stood in the far back with some of the ladies' maids she
had met. Tomas sought out Aislin, and found a spot

near the side of the hall so he didn't block the view of too many people.

Aislin didn't really get a chance to look around until she was standing beside Tomas waiting for the ceremony to start. She noticed then that the garlands and bouquets of flowers decorating the hall were all shades of pink. Pale pink, dark pink, dusky pink, and bright pink blossoms covered nearly every surface. It was almost as if the pink-loving fairy, Dianthus, had splashed her favorite-colored dust everywhere, turning it all pink. Unfortunately, Aislin had chosen to wear her new pink gown. It was a lovely dress and looked beautiful on her, which was why she had worn it, but it made her blend into the wall behind her. When she looked around, she realized that not a single other person was wearing pink. She also noticed the amused glances people were casting her way.

"Did everyone else know that all the flowers were going to be pink?" she asked Tomas.

"I didn't," he said. "But then, I'm not from Morain. Just a minute and I'll ask."

Aislin shook her head and was about to tell him not to bother when he turned and whispered to the middle-aged woman on his other side. The woman smiled when she whispered back, and glanced pointedly at Aislin.

"She said that it's tradition to decorate in pink and not to wear pink when a princess is born in the royal household of Morain," Tomas told Aislin. "It's a lot harder to find blue flowers when it's a boy, so they decorate with blue banners instead. Even then, you don't wear blue."

"It would have been nice if someone had told me," said Aislin.

"From what I've seen, there aren't too many nice people in Morain," Tomas replied. Even though he was trying to speak quietly, the woman on his other side scowled.

Aislin was still thinking about her dress when the ceremony started. With all the people standing in front of her, she couldn't see anything. She couldn't hear anything either, so she didn't know it was over until people began to whisper and look around the room.

"What happens next?" Aislin asked Tomas.

"Gifts, I think," he said, looking over the heads of the people around them. "They're waiting for . . . Ah, there she is."

"There who is?" Aislin asked, standing on her

tiptoes. When she still couldn't see anything, she began to get frustrated, especially when the people blocking her view started to get excited.

Suddenly she felt it, the familiar tingle that meant a fairy was nearby. It wasn't Poppy either, because she was still standing way in the back. Although Aislin was certain that she had to be mistaken, she couldn't shake the feeling that the person they were all watching was a fairy.

"I need to see this," she said, but Tomas was watching whatever was going on as eagerly as the other people in the crowd and didn't seem to hear her.

Aislin looked around. There had to be somewhere she could go. No one was standing beyond the pillar, so maybe... When Aislin spotted the spikes holding up the garlands, she knew what she had to do. Having spent many hours climbing trees and rocks with her friends, climbing a pillar would be easy.

Tomas didn't seem to notice when Aislin left him to squeeze past the people between her and the pillar. When she reached its base, she grabbed hold of one of the spikes on the side where no one was standing and pulled herself up. Finding hand and foot supports, she climbed up the pillar until she could see what was going on.

Aislin gasped. She was so shocked that she almost lost her footing. It was a fairy, all right, even though that wasn't supposed to be possible in the human kingdoms. With her blue hair and pointed ears, she was obviously a flower fairy, just like the ones Aislin had often seen at home, although not nearly as well kept or as pretty. The fairy wore a blue gown made of overlapping petals with a green vine belt. Her gown reminded Aislin of morning glories, although the color was a little faded.

Aislin watched as King Tyburr approached the fairy, carrying a small wooden chest. When he handed it to her, she opened it right away, and poked around inside it. Satisfied with what she'd found, she walked past the king and queen to the cradle on the dais, held her hand over the baby inside, and sprinkled sparkling fairy dust on her. The baby sneezed, making everyone laugh. People had begun to applaud when the fairy turned to leave. She stopped suddenly, her eyes narrowing as she looked toward the back of the hall. Aislin guessed she had sensed Poppy.

Aislin pressed herself against the garlands of flowers just as the fairy turned and looked in her direction. This new fairy might not be able to sense that Aislin was part fairy, but she could tell that someone *different* was on that side of the room. When the fairy's gaze swept over her and moved on, Aislin was glad that she blended in so well with the decorations. The fairy appeared to be unsettled when she turned and fled the room.

Aislin hurried down off the pillar and pushed between the milling people to reach Tomas. "What just happened?" she asked him.

"The fairy gave the princess her christening gift," said Tomas, nonchalant. "I assume it will be the gift of beauty, like most princesses get. Don't they do that in your kingdom?"

Aislin was shocked. "You know about *fairies*?"

"Of course!" said Tomas. "Doesn't everyone? I know there aren't very many, but everyone knows who they are. That was Morning Glory. She's invited to a lot of christenings."

Aislin wasn't sure what to say. There weren't supposed to be any fairies outside the land between the mountains. Her whole life, she'd been told that they had all left the human kingdoms. How was this even possible?

And there was something else that she didn't understand. "Did the king pay her?"

Tomas nodded. "That's how it's always done. The

infant's father pays the fairy, who bestows one gift. It's usually beauty for girls, although boys can receive a handsome appearance, bravery, or skill with weapons. My father isn't a king, but he could still afford a gift for me. He asked a fairy that was passing through at the time. She didn't give me what he expected, though, and he's always been sorry he did it."

"What did the fairy give you?" Aislin asked.

"The gift of truth, of course," said Tomas. "You didn't think I wanted to tell the truth whenever I opened my mouth, did you? Sometimes it's the last thing I want to do. If I didn't have this gift, Tyburr wouldn't have had me brought here so he could interrogate me about my father. But there's something he doesn't know; I learned long ago to keep my mouth shut when I didn't want the truth to come out. I talk only when I have something I want to say."

Chapter 13

AISLIN DIDN'T KNOW WHAT to think. There were fairies in the human world and they were freely interacting with humans! The fact that they were getting paid to do it only made it worse. Fairy history was filled with stories of fairies dealing with humans, but the fairies had always used their magic to help them as a favor or reward, not for payment! It wasn't even something that most normal fairies would consider!

Aislin drifted at Tomas's side as the celebration continued, thinking about what it meant to have fairies living among the humans. So much for the humans thinking that fairies were a myth! She wondered for a moment if her parents or grandparents were aware that some fairies had been left behind, but immediately rejected the idea. If they knew, they never would have worked so hard to keep secret their presence in the land between the mountains. And they would surely have sought out the other fairies long ago.

Aislin needed to send word to the fey. Her fairy grandparents would have to decide what to do; Aislin was certain that this knowledge was going to change everything. She'd have to send another message by bird.

Aislin was looking around for Poppy when Craiger entered the hall. He went straight to the king and they stood together deep in conversation. After a few minutes, the king spoke to the queen, who snatched the baby from the cradle and ran from the room. Aislin watched as King Tyburr called for the pages. The young boys dashed up to the dais to receive their instructions, then one boy ran to Selene, and one ran to Rory. Aislin was surprised when a third searched the crowd until he found her and Tomas.

"You're both to come with me," he told them, and started for the door.

"Where are we going?" Tomas asked as he and Aislin hurried after the page.

"The courtyard," the page said. "Don't ask me anything else, because that's all I know."

When Aislin glanced at Tomas, he shrugged and shook his head. Something had happened, but they'd have to wait to find out what it was exactly. Curious, they followed the page as he raced through the corridor. When they finally reached the courtyard, they found two carriages waiting at the bottom of the steps. Mounted soldiers were lined up behind them, and other soldiers were positioned at the door to each carriage.

"You're to go in this carriage, Your Highness," a soldier told Aislin as he pointed at the one in front.

"Where are we going?" she asked, but he just reached for her hand to help her up the step.

When she turned to Tomas, a soldier was already directing him to the other carriage where she could see Rory peering out. Frowning, she climbed into hers. When she stepped inside, she was dismayed to see Selene and four of her ladies-in-waiting already taking up most of the space.

"I told you she was going to ride with us," said Merrilee. "That's why Natalie couldn't come, too."

The moment the door closed behind Aislin, the

carriage began to move. Joselle and Laneece grudgingly moved to make room for her on the seat.

"What's going on?" asked Aislin as she tried to wedge herself against the side of the vehicle. "Why did we have to leave so suddenly?"

"King Ozwalt's troops have landed in the port and are advancing on the castle," Selene announced, eager to share the news. "Father is sending Rory and me to safety at one of his estates."

Aislin shifted around to look out the window. They had crossed through the gateway and were turning onto a street that headed away from the port. People were running down the street shouting, and more of King Tyburr's soldiers were already trooping past. The girls looked at each other nervously as they rumbled through the city, not even slowing as they passed through one gate after another. It wasn't until they had left the city behind them and could see farms and woodland ahead that they began to relax.

Selene was chatting with Merrilee when Aislin asked, "What about the others?"

"What others?" asked Selene. "Queen Tatya and the baby left before we did."

"I meant the servants," Aislin told her. "Aren't they coming, too?"

Laneece and Merrilee laughed. "Are you that worried about finding someone to brush your hair and help you change your clothes?" asked Joselle. "I'm sure we'll find someone to help you, even if it's the scullery maid."

"That isn't it at all," Aislin replied. "I just want to make sure that they're all right." She hated leaving Poppy and Twinket behind and wouldn't have if she could have prevented it. She'd just have to hope that her friends would be fine without her.

Aislin glanced at Selene. The girl was beautiful, which made sense if a fairy had given her the gift of beauty as a christening gift. If her appearance had changed drastically, it would explain why she didn't look like either of her parents.

When Merrilee leaned closer to Selene and whispered something, the princess looked at her sharply and said, "That wasn't very nice. I told you before that I don't want to hear you say things like that."

Merrilee sat back in her seat, looking like a small child who had just been scolded.

Turning toward the window again, Aislin watched the scenery evolve from farmland into forest. At first the trees were well-spaced, evidence that a woodcutter had been busy, but as they continued on, the trees grew closer together and the shadows became deeper.

They rode through the day and into the night, trying to sleep as much as they could in the lurching, bouncing carriage. The sun was just starting to come up when suddenly the carriage stopped with a jolt, sending two of the girls tumbling to the floor. "What was that?" Selene cried as Merrilee and Laneece tried to untangle themselves and return to their seats.

Aislin was peering out the window, hoping to see what might have caused their sudden stop, when she heard shouting and the clash of swords. After a few minutes, soldiers wearing crossed-sword insignia approached the door. She sat back, not sure what to do, when the men yanked the door beside her open. "Get out!" one of them ordered.

"What is the meaning of this?" asked Selene in an imperious tone.

A soldier dressed like an officer appeared in the doorway. "Which one of you is the princess Selene?"

The girls froze and not one of them looked at Selene.

Aislin looked around for the other carriage, but it wasn't behind them as she'd thought. She hoped Tomas had gotten away.

"Get them out of there so we can talk to them," the officer told his men.

Aislin was closest to the door and didn't balk when a soldier gestured to her. As she climbed down, she could hear the girls whispering. More than one of them mentioned her name. Selene was arguing with them in harsh whispers right until she started to get out. When they were standing there, huddled together, the officer asked again, "Which one of you is Princess Selene?"

Aislin gasped when the four ladies-in-waiting turned and pointed at her. "That's her," said Merrilee.

"That's her, all right," said Laneece. "Don't believe her if she says she isn't. She's a liar."

"That's not Princess Selene," said Selene. "I am."

"Don't try to give yourself up for the princess!" said Merrilee. "She doesn't deserve your sacrifice."

Aislin glanced at Selene. The princess was willing to betray herself even though the other girls were trying to protect her. Aislin was touched that the princess didn't want to go along with their lies and endanger her. But, although she had no idea why these men wanted Selene, Aislin knew that she could handle whatever they had planned better than a human girl.

"I'm Selene," she stated.

The other girls looked surprised. "No, she's—" Selene began, until Laneece jabbed her with her elbow.

"Put her on the horse and tie her hands," the officer said, pointing at Aislin.

Aislin followed the men without protest. One of the soldiers led her to a horse and boosted her into the saddle. When he tied her hands, he did it loosely enough that she could still manage the reins.

They left her there with her horse tied to the front of the carriage. The vehicle shifted and she heard the sound of pounding on wood. When it ended, the soldiers came for Aislin and led her horse past the carriage back the way they had come. She could see now what they'd been doing; they had removed a wheel and broken it, tossing the bigger pieces into the forest. When she saw Selene and her ladies-in-waiting sitting on the side of the road, the princess started to stand, but the girls on either side of her pulled her back down again.

Taking all the horses with them, the soldiers escorted Aislin down the road. She had no idea where they were taking her and was surprised to spot the second carriage with Tomas, Rory, and another group of soldiers beside it.

"We can go now," said the officer who had taken Aislin. "We got the princess Selene."

"Where?" said Rory, looking behind them. "I don't see her."

The soldiers looked at each other, confused.

Tomas shook his head. "This isn't Selene," he said, and started to undo Aislin's hands. "This is my friend, Princess Aislin."

"I didn't know why they wanted Selene. I thought I could handle whatever came better than she could, so I told them that I was Selene," Aislin said as he helped her down from the horse's back. "Do you know these men?"

"I do," said Tomas. "They're my father's men and I'd trust them with my life, but apparently they aren't very good at discerning the truth."

The soldiers looked embarrassed, but it was the officer who said, "We left the real Princess Selene back with the carriage. We can ride back there and fetch her."

"There isn't time," said Tomas. "One of Tyburr's children will be enough. Take Prince Rory and get going. The other carriages will be coming soon. I want to be long gone before they arrive."

"What about me?" Rory asked as the soldiers led him to a horse. "I'm your friend, too!"

"You were never my friend, which you made plain

every day I was in your castle," Tomas told him before turning to the officer. "You might want to gag him. He has a very unpleasant personality."

"What about Princess Aislin?" asked the officer.

"That's for her to decide," said Tomas.

Taking Aislin's hand, he led her away from the others to a spot where Rory couldn't hear them. "I couldn't tell you about my mission before, but I can now," said Tomas. "The men came for me so that I could do what I need to do. If you go with me, I'll return you to your own kingdom afterward. I have no idea what dangers we might encounter, so it won't be an easy trip. However, if you'd prefer, you could go back to Scarmander, which is where the men are taking Rory to hold just as his father held me. If you go with them, you'll be safe, but it might be some time before I'll be able to take you home. The choice is yours."

Aislin needed to know more. "What is this mission?" she asked.

"I'm taking a gift to the fairy Baibre in the wildest part of these very woods," Tomas told her. "The gift is from Baibre's twin sister, who is hoping for a reconciliation. If Baibre accepts the gift, the fairies will stay out of the war and the kings will meet to settle their differences. If she doesn't accept it, we might be in for a long and bloody war. So, which will it be? Do you want to go with me, or Rory?"

"I'm going with you," said Aislin. "And I'll help you if I can."

Tomas laughed. "I'm not sure how much a princess could help me!"

"I'm not just a princess," Aislin said. "There are things you don't know about me, but before I tell you, you have to promise not to tell anyone else."

Tomas looked perplexed. "I promise," he replied.

"I'm part fairy ...," Aislin told him.

Tomas laughed. "You mean you can make yourself small and fly away?"

Aislin shook her head. "No, I can't do that."

"Then you can change people with magic! Why didn't you turn Selene's friends into insects or something when you had the chance?"

"I can't do that either," said Aislin. "But there are other things I can do that humans can't."

"This isn't the time for jokes, Aislin," Tomas told her. "This mission is important."

"I understand that, and I'm not joking," she told him. "You'll see."

Aislin would go with him, but it wasn't that she wanted to help him with his mission as much as that she wanted to meet the fairy Baibre. It was time she learned all she could about the fairies her grandparents had left behind.

Chapter 14

RORY STARTED COMPLAINING AS soon as they put him on a horse, so the soldiers took Tomas's advice and gagged the Prince of Morain. The group split in two, with the larger contingent taking all the horses back across the border. Two soldiers named Cadby and Marden went with Tomas and Aislin to find the fairy. Cadby wasn't much older than Tomas, but Marden already had a few gray hairs.

"Do you have a map?" Aislin asked as they started walking down the road.

"No, but I do have directions," said Tomas. "We have to look for landmarks. The first one is a pile of rocks that roughly resembles a sleeping cat. It's up here a little way. I saw it out of the carriage window when we drove past. Ah, there it is. We turn here and go due east."

They left the road then, being careful not to leave a trail into the woods. It was the first time Aislin had walked in the woods since leaving Eliasind and she loved it. She listened to the birds gossiping, the squirrels complaining, and the smaller creatures rustling in the underbrush. The shade of the deep forest felt like home, and she couldn't help but look for the familiar beings within the branches. She was disappointed when she failed to see nymphs peeking out at her from trees, sprites blowing dandelion puffs, or gnomes carrying sacks of freshly picked mushrooms.

After walking for three quarters of an hour, they reached a steep drop-off. Tomas stopped to look around. "We're looking for a waterfall and we should have found it well before now. I was told that it was about a mile from the sleeping-cat rock."

"We headed due east, just like your directions said," Cadby told him. "Maybe your directions were wrong."

"The waterfall is probably where a stream or river plunges over this drop-off," said Marden. "It should be around here somewhere. I think we should split up.

Two of us should go north and two should go south. We can meet back here in an hour."

"We're not splitting up," said Tomas. "There's no telling what lives in this forest, so we need to stay together. And this is way too far from where we started. We probably passed the waterfall already. We'll retrace our steps and this time we'll listen carefully for moving water."

They turned around and started back, stopping now and then to listen, but no one saw or heard a waterfall. All too soon, they spotted the sleeping-cat rock again.

Tomas sighed. "We'll just have to keep looking. That waterfall has to be here somewhere. Let's spread out this time, but not so far that we can't see each other."

They tried Tomas's new approach, but found themselves back at the drop-off again. He was trying to decide what to do next when Aislin noticed a pebble on the ground. Perhaps it was time she started to help. Tomas and Marden were debating where they should go next when Aislin picked up the pebble. Closing her eyes, she let her mind sink into the tiny rock. Although it would have looked like an ordinary piece of granite to anyone else, to a pedrasi it was a doorway into another world. The little piece of stone talked to her, not with words, but with impressions and images. When she thought about where she wanted to go, the pebble linked up with all the other stones in the area, showing her where water tumbled over them. Some visions showed her the courses of rivers that had worn away at the bedrock for centuries, while others showed her newly diverted streams that had only just begun to cool the stones' sun-heated surfaces.

When Aislin found a waterfall that wasn't far away, she wondered how to get there. Inexplicably, the images went murky and indistinct.

Aislin sighed. Even for a pedrasi princess, reading stone wasn't always easy. Her thoughts now slid to someone who could help her, someone who could tell her how to find the waterfall she sought.

Tomas didn't notice when Aislin slipped between the trees and made her way through ferns and bracken to an old tree stump. When she saw the faint outline of a door cut into the bark, she knelt down and gave it three gentle raps.

The door opened suddenly and a gnome with a long white beard and bushy eyebrows popped his head out. "All right, all right!" he grumbled. "There's no need to break my door down! Who are you and what do you want?"

"Directions, if you don't mind, kind sir," Aislin told the gnome. "I'm looking for a waterfall, but can't find it anywhere. Would you please tell me how to reach it?"

The gnome squinted up at her while rubbing the side of his nose with his finger. He frowned and tilted his head to the side, still studying her. Suddenly he reached out and touched her hand where it rested on her knee. The gnome gasped and looked up at her face, as if seeing something new and completely unexpected.

"Fairy royalty!" he cried. "But that's not all. You're something else, too, I just can't tell what."

Aislin nodded. "I'm half fairy and half pedrasi," she replied.

"Pedrasi! We don't see your kind around here," said the gnome. "Not many fairies either, but I've seen only one pedrasi my entire life and that was when I was visiting my uncle who lives by the Whitestone Mountains. I thought pedrasi loved the mountains and never left them."

"That's true of most of them," Aislin told him. "My grandparents have never ventured out of their mountain home, not even when their daughter married my father. They weren't happy when my mother left."

"And here you are!" the gnome exclaimed. "My wife will be sorry she visited friends today and wasn't here to meet you. What can I do for you, Princess? Oh, right! The waterfall. Are you traveling alone?"

Aislin shook her head. "I'm with some human men. Don't worry, I came to see you without them," she said when the gnome started looking around nervously.

"Then they're probably armed," he told her. "You'll never find that waterfall from here. There's a spell on this side of the forest. Anyone who carries weapons will be lost and never get where they want to go. The only thing you'll find is the way back to where you started, which is precisely where you need to be. Return to where you began looking and make the humans leave their weapons behind. After that, you'll find the waterfall easily enough."

"Thank you. You've been very helpful," said Aislin.

"You're welcome, Your Highness," the gnome replied. "It was a real pleasure meeting a fairy-pedrasi princess. I can't wait to tell my wife. She is going to be so jealous!"

When Aislin returned to Tomas, he was still talking to the men. "We have to go back to where we started," she told him. "It's the only way we'll find the waterfall."

"We've already done that," Marden grumbled.

"Not like this," said Aislin.

"What do you think we should do differently?" asked Tomas.

Aislin glanced at his men, then at Tomas. "I need to speak with you privately for a moment," she told Tomas. "If you want my help, you'll come with me."

His eyes met hers for an instant. He nodded and said to his men, "We'll be right back."

After walking far enough that the men couldn't hear them, Aislin turned to Tomas. "I just spoke with a gnome who told me what we have to do to find the waterfall. If you want to find it, you need to listen to me, unless you've come up with a better idea."

Tomas gave her an odd look. "I don't have any reason to doubt you, so we might as well try what you suggest. But tell me, if part of you is fairy, is the rest of you human? Are you really a princess?"

Aislin smiled. "I have no human blood, but I really am a princess. My parents and my grandparents are all royalty."

"If you're part fairy, you're so much more than a princess!" said Tomas. "I wish Rory and those girls at the castle knew just who they were mocking! What did this gnome tell you?"

"We have to return to the sleeping-cat rock and leave our weapons there," said Aislin. "As long as we have weapons with us, we'll never find Baibre."

Tomas glanced at the position of the sun in the sky. "Then we need to get started. We've already wasted a good part of the day walking back and forth."

They knew the way back to the sleeping-cat rock so well that it didn't take them long to reach it. The only difficulty came when Tomas told the men that they'd have to leave their weapons behind. "But we'll need them," said Marden. "I saw the marks of bear claws on a tree. What if we encounter a bear?"

"I saw a strange feather that couldn't have come from any bird," Cadby told them. "There are danger-ous creatures in these woods. We need our weapons."

"The animals won't hurt us," Aislin reassured them.

"You might believe that, Your Highness, but I don't," said Marden. "I'm not going anywhere without my crossbow and knife."

"Then I think you men should stay here and wait for us," said Aislin. "Keep well back from the road and rest. We shouldn't be long now."

"I don't like this," Cadby mumbled as Tomas and Aislin walked off.

They had retraced their steps only partway when they found that things didn't look quite the same. The trees weren't in the same places, the underbrush was lusher, and there was a well-defined path that they hadn't seen before. "Do you think that heads toward the waterfall?" Tomas asked Aislin.

She shrugged. "It is going due east and it doesn't have any magic to trap or trick us. We should be safe enough."

"You can sense magic?" asked Tomas.

"Usually, although my father is much better at it," she replied.

"Then your father is a fairy?" Tomas asked her. "What's your mother?"

"A kind and lovely woman," Aislin told him. "She's pedrasi and has her own set of skills. I'm more like her than I am my father."

"I've never heard of pedrasi," said Tomas.

"I doubt there are many humans who have," Aislin replied. "Pedrasi tend to keep to themselves." She glanced at the trees around them, then back at Tomas. "I think we should take the path. We'll leave it if it varies from where we want to go."

"All right," said Tomas, "but please tell me if you feel magic or see anything odd. I may not have a weapon, but I'm not completely helpless."

Aislin couldn't help but smile to herself. She wasn't all that helpless either.

They took the path, which wound between trees while still heading east. Aislin heard the waterfall first and started walking faster. "It's just ahead," she told Tomas.

"How do you know that?" he asked. "I don't hear it."

"No, but I do," said Aislin. "It isn't far."

Tomas frowned and hurried to catch up. When he finally heard it, he quickened his pace even more. They reached the edge of a small lake at the base of the falls only minutes later. Tomas frowned and bent down to examine the ground. "Do you see all these paw prints?

It looks as if a lot of animals come here to drink. We need to be careful."

"We will be," said Aislin. "What are we supposed to look for next? Do you know what she lives in?"

"I was told that we'd find it once we reached the waterfall. What do fairies usually live in anyway?"

"That depends," Aislin told him as she looked around. "I live in a castle, but I know fairies who live in flowers, and some who live in caves. Others live in large cottages or one-room huts. I don't see any cottages or huts. Do you see anything that might be the opening of a cave? It will take us a lot longer to find her if she lives in a flower."

"No caves so far," he told her as he continued to look.

Aislin paused, sensing that someone was watching her. When she turned, she saw a man's face peering out from among the foliage.

"Don't look now, but we have company," she told Tomas.

"Did you find the fairy?" he asked, trying to see where she was looking.

Aislin shook her head. "No, actually it's someone very different. Stand absolutely still and let me talk to him."

191

"Is that a man?" Tomas asked, studying the deep shadows.

The creature turned its head, focusing on Tomas. Wiggling its haunches, it bounded from the underbrush and landed only yards away, revealing its lion body and wicked, scorpion tail. When it opened its wide mouth, Aislin could see three rows of very sharp teeth inside. Its roar was like the blast of a trumpet and made both Aislin and Tomas clap their hands over their ears.

"That's a manticore!" Tomas cried. "Quick, Aislin, get behind me." Bending down, he grabbed a broken branch from the ground and held it like a club.

But then an ear-splitting screech came from overhead. Leaves and small twigs rained down on Aislin and Tomas as a griffin descended from the sky between the overarching branches. The griffin landed in front of the manticore, hissing and clacking its eagle-like beak. Its lion tail twitched and the muscles in its lion body quivered. With another trumpet blast, the manticore leaped onto the griffin, sending them both tumbling across the ground, raking each other with tooth, beak, and claw. It was hard to tell where one lion body ended and the other began. Tomas grabbed Aislin around the waist and dragged her out of the way.

"No!" Aislin told him, struggling to get free.

"We need to get out of here!" Tomas told her.

"No, I need to end this!" she cried. Letting herself go limp, she slipped from his arms and landed on the ground with her hand on a large, flat rock. Aislin closed her eyes, and focused on pulling strength from the rock into herself. Instead of directing the power into her arms, she raised her head, opened her eyes and sent the power out through her voice, shouting, "Stop fighting!"

The manticore and the griffin immediately rolled apart. Their hackles were down and their ears perked up when they turned and approached her, purring. Tomas's jaw dropped when the two fearsome beasts began to rub against Aislin like a couple of oversized housecats. When Aislin scratched them behind their ears, their purring grew even louder.

"Why were you fighting?" Aislin asked the manticore.

"I saw the human first," said the manticore, and his hackles started to rise again. "He's mine to eat, not the griffin's."

"He's no one's to eat and is not to be touched," Aislin told him. "The human is my friend and companion. Do you know who I am?"

The manticore bowed his head. "I heard it in your voice and saw it in your eyes. You are one of the magic ones that left long ago, yet you are different. How can that be?"

"I am a child of the old ones," said Aislin. "My grandparents ruled the fey, and your kind as well. I require your help now, not your fighting."

"What may we do for you, Your Highness?" the manticore asked, bowing so that its chin touched the ground. Taking his cue from the manticore, the griffin also bowed. "Birdbrain here will help you as well," the manticore added.

"At this time, all I need are directions," Aislin told them. "I'm looking for the home of the fairy Baibre."

"Look up," said the manticore.

Aislin did, and saw the tree house right away. It was larger than a good-sized cottage and filled the branches of one of the bigger trees.

"There's a door in the trunk," the manticore told her. "Be careful. Baibre doesn't like visitors."

"I understand, and thank you," Aislin told them. "And next time, don't be so eager to eat a human. My kind considered them friends."

"Baibre is our friend. She raised me from a cub and him from a hatchling to be her protectors. She wants us to eat intruders," said the manticore. "She says it keeps the riffraff away. But if it displeases Your Highness, we won't do it anymore. Although, it was my turn."

The griffin screeched, but Aislin interrupted before they could get into another tussle. "It was nice to meet you, and I thank you again for your help. You may go now."

She didn't move until the griffin and the manticore had disappeared back into the forest. When she could no longer sense them, she turned to the tree and began to walk around the trunk. She found a door standing slightly ajar on the other side.

"I can't believe that worked!" Tomas said, still searching the forest with his eyes.

"I treated them with respect and they returned in kind," said Aislin. "Sometimes being polite is all it takes."

Chapter 15

THE DOOR CREAKED LOUDLY as Aislin pushed it open. She shrugged and glanced at Tomas. "After the racket the manticore and the griffin made, we weren't going to sneak in anyway." When she peered inside, there wasn't much to see other than a set of steep, narrow stairs that wound up the inside of the trunk. Knotholes let in the only light.

Tomas had to bend down to look inside. "Let me go first," he said, and slipped into the trunk.

Although his shoulders brushed both sides of the narrow space, he climbed up the stairs like a squirrel up a tree. It wasn't as easy for Aislin. Her legs were much shorter than his and the steps were so steep that taking each one was an effort. She knew when he reached the top because his footsteps grew silent and all she could hear was her own breathing.

Irritated with herself for being so short, and with Tomas for being so fast, she tried to hurry. When she finally reached the top, she was out of breath and it took her a moment to understand what she was seeing.

The tree house appeared to be one large room with a single high ceiling and the floor broken up into different levels. Branches grew through the floor and up through the roof. Nests were tucked into every nook and cranny and birds of all sorts flew in and out through the window openings, while squirrels chittered at Aislin from the branches. One squirrel was perched on a small table, cracking nuts. Another was staring at a shape wrapped in spiderwebs with a large snake wrapped around its middle. At first Aislin didn't realize that the shape was really Tomas.

She gasped and ran over to her friend. The snake was squeezing so hard that Tomas's face was turning blue. "Stop that right now!" she shouted. The snake ignored her and kept squeezing.

Aislin glanced at her hand, wanting to draw more

power from the stone, but she must have dropped it. Hoping to find another, she let her gaze dart around the room. When she didn't see anything she could use right away, she grabbed hold of the snake, trying to pull it off. "Let go!" she cried, but the snake just hissed at her.

A crow flew through the window and landed on one of the larger nests. It dropped something shiny and began rearranging things. Aislin's head snapped around when she sensed stone buried among the crow's collection of treasures. She had to climb partway up the tree, and wave one arm at the crow to fend it off, but she soon found a rock embedded with a shiny bit of mica. It wasn't much, but it was enough. Jumping down from her perch, she drew on the strength of the stone, releasing it in her voice. "I order you to let him go!"

The snake hissed at her even as it relaxed its coils and dropped to the floor. Tomas sighed and his head lolled, but she could still see the rise and fall of his chest through the mass of spiderwebs that held him upright.

A white-haired fairy dressed in gray cobwebs stepped out of the shadows. The lines in her face were etched so deeply that she reminded Aislin of the dried-apple dolls that her nursemaid, Larch, used to make for her. "Who are you to order my snake to do any-thing?" the fairy asked.

"I am Princess Aislin of the royal house of Eliasind, and the combined houses of Fairengar and Deephold," said Aislin.

The fairy laughed and looked Aislin up and down. "You dredge up names from long ago. Fairengar is no more and Deephold was but a legend. I've never heard of a kingdom named Eliasind. You lie, and I don't like liars."

"And I don't like people who doubt my word," said Aislin. "But if you need proof, you shall have it." Remembering how the gnome had recognized her for what she was by touch, she reached for the fairy's hand. She had enough power coursing through her to send a jolt into Baibre. A quick indrawn breath and a widen-ing of the fairy's eyes told Aislin that touching her had worked.

"You're a fairy and a pedrasi! I could sense your royal blood," the fairy said, her face turning pale.

"My father's parents are King Darinar and Queen Surinen of Fairengar. My mother is the daughter of King Talus and Queen Amethyst, pedrasi rulers of Deephold in the Whitestone Mountains," Aislin proclaimed in a ringing voice.

The fairy knelt in front of Aislin, her head bowed. "What do you want of me, Your Highness?"

"Release him now," Aislin said, gesturing to Tomas.

With a wave of the fairy's hand, the spiderwebs shattered as if they were made of glass. Tomas collapsed, limp and seemingly boneless. His hand twitched, but he didn't get up.

"You need to learn some manners," said Aislin. "This young man brought you a gift. You had no right to treat him as you did. Fairies do not act this way. My grandparents would be appalled!"

Baibre straightened her back, outrage plain on her face. "Fairies learn to do what they must when they are alone with no fairy neighbors to count on, and no defense against the humans but their own wits! I was abandoned when I was young and didn't know where to turn. I did what I needed to do to survive. Where were the king and queen of the fairies when I needed them, or their warriors when villagers chased my sister and me from our home? We couldn't even find our own parents when we went looking for them!"

"No one was supposed to be left behind," said Aislin. "My grandparents did everything they could to make sure that didn't happen."

"But it did! And it wasn't long before the humans learned that the fairy royalty had disappeared. Hunting parties came looking for us, thinking they would take us captive to keep us from leaving as well. They tried to make us do their will, and use our magic as they wished. Instead we used our magic to escape and hide from them. Some fairies withered away, lonely and forgotten, while others nurtured their magic and became powerful enough to stand against anyone who opposed them. I came here to live, and used my magic to keep hunters at bay."

"I'm sorry," Aislin told her, "but the king and queen didn't know that anyone was left behind."

"How could they not know?" Baibre cried. "Didn't they ask if anyone was missing? Surely my parents knew that my sister and I weren't there!"

"I wasn't born yet, but I have read the histories," said Aislin. "Some fairies kept to themselves and went straight into the wilderness after the crossing. It's hard to count fairies who don't want to be counted."

Baibre looked away, and shrugged. "We were a solitary lot. My parents were never very social. Tell me, what is this gift he brought? Why would a young human bring me a gift?"

Aislin glanced at Tomas. "He was delivering it for your sister. You have to wake him if you want it. I don't know where or what it is."

"I don't need magic for that," Baibre declared. Grabbing a bucket from a bench in the back of the room, she tossed water on Tomas, drenching him until he sat up, spluttering.

"What's going on?" he asked Aislin.

"Baibre and I have been talking," she replied. "How are your ribs?"

"Sore," he said, rubbing his rib cage. "But not too bad. What happened to the snake?"

"It left," said Baibre. "Tell me, young man, what did you bring me?"

Tomas scrambled to his feet and reached into the neck of his tunic. Pulling out a golden chain, he drew it over his head and held it out to Baibre. Light glinted off the filigree and crystal locket that hung from the end of the chain. Aislin thought she saw a golden stone inside. "This is from your sister, Aghamonda. She wanted me to tell you that she hopes it will heal the rift between you and that she'll see you soon."

"Did she really?" Baibre said, reaching out to take it. "We parted under unpleasant circumstances years ago. I never thought she'd be the one to make the first move to reconcile. This is lovely. Look, the locket opens. Is that amber?"

Aislin couldn't sense amber the way she could stone born of the earth. She stepped closer to see it better and was only a few feet away when Baibre opened the locket, releasing a pale green mist. The moment the mist touched Baibre's face, a crack of thunder and a bolt of bright light knocked both Aislin and Tomas off their feet.

Tomas sat up first, rubbing his head and looking around. When he saw Aislin lying on the floor beside him, he jumped up and reached for her hand. "Are you all right?"

Aislin nodded. "I think so."

Tomas was pulling her to her feet when he said, "Baibre's gone. I don't know what happened."

"Is that her locket?" Aislin asked, pointing at something by Tomas's feet.

When he bent down to pick it up, she took it from him and peered at the amber. It looked different now, and she thought she saw something moving inside. She gasped and almost dropped the locket. Something *was* moving, something that wanted to get out. A very tiny, frantic-looking Baibre was pounding on the locket from the inside.

"I know what happened to Baibre!" Aislin cried. "She was sucked into the amber when she touched it. The magic must have been dormant until then. Aghamonda didn't want you to deliver a gift! She wanted you to deliver a trap that her sister couldn't resist!"

Chapter 16

TOMAS LOOKED APPALLED. "I didn't know! I never met Aghamonda; I just know what my father told me when he asked me to bring the locket to Baibre. I believed him when he said it was a gift. I am so sorry!" he said to the tiny face inside the swinging locket. "I never would have given it to you if I'd known!"

"Don't blame your father. He probably didn't know either," said Aislin. She examined the locket, turning it over in her hand. "We can't just leave it here for some-one to find. I'd free her if I could, but I don't have the magic to undo this. Not many fairies do. My father and his parents could, though. We'll have to take it with us."

When she tried to give the locket back to Tomas, he pushed her hand away. "I can't look at that thing."

"Then I'll carry it," said Aislin, and she slipped the chain over her head.

"I think my father did know," said Tomas. "Because now the rest of what he said makes sense. He said that if Baibre doesn't tell me not to, I'm to take the locket back to Aghamonda. I couldn't figure out that part until now. I mean, why would you give someone a gift, then take it back right away? But Baibre can't tell me not to if she's trapped inside it. Why do you think Aghamonda wanted to trap her sister like this?"

"I'm not sure, but it can't be for anything good," said Aislin. "I don't think you should give it to her."

"I won't," said Tomas. "Anyone who would do this to her sister can't be a good person. What do you want to do next? You helped me, and it's time for me to live up to my part of the bargain. I said I'd take you home after we gave Baibre the gift. Are you ready to go?"

Aislin wanted to say yes. From the moment she'd left her family's castle with King Tyburr, all she'd wanted was to go back home. She'd dreamed about it every night when she fell asleep, and thought about it a dozen times every day. The word was on the tip of her tongue, but she knew she couldn't, not yet at least. Something was going on with the fairies who'd been left behind.

Her grandparents needed to know about it, and Aislin was the only one who could help.

"I think I'd rather go to Scarmander with you instead. I'd like to meet this fairy, Aghamonda. She's up to something and I want to know what she's planning."

"All right," Tomas told her. "But I have to warn you, I've heard that she's very intimidating."

Aislin laughed. "She can't possibly be more intimidating than my grandparents, but thanks for the warning."

Tomas and Aislin headed toward the sleeping-cat rock and found the two soldiers among the trees not far from the road. Cadby was asleep on his back with his mouth open, snoring softly, but Marden was whittling and he saw them right away. "How did it go?" asked Marden.

"I did what I was sent to do," Tomas told him, looking grim. "Let's go. I want to put this place behind us as soon as possible."

"King Tyburr's men passed by a while ago," Marden said as he tucked his knife into his belt. "We heard shouting, but they haven't been back this way since."

"We'll make our best time if we stick to the road for as long as we can. Be alert for horses and riders!" Tomas told them.

Aislin glanced back as they approached the dirt road. Although she couldn't see them, she could sense that two beings were following her. She was sure they weren't any of King Tyburr's men. From the feeling she got, they were more likely the manticore and the griffin.

Aislin and Tomas walked without talking, listening for the sounds of someone's approach. Dust puffed around their feet, clouding the narrow band of sunlight that brightened the center of the road. A snake that had been warming itself slithered into the underbrush at their approach. Something big enough to make the trees shake lumbered off when they drew close. They hadn't gone far when Aislin heard a cry for help coming from the woods on the far side of the road.

"Twinket!" she cried, recognizing the doll's voice. Alarmed, she ran into the woods without waiting for the others.

"What's a Twinket?" asked Cadby.

"I have no idea," Tomas replied as they took off after Aislin.

Aislin followed the doll's cries deep into the woods,

stopping only when she saw the reason Twinket was screaming. Seven trolls—long-armed, lumpy, and not much taller than the princess herself—had found the doll. Aislin had never seen a troll before, but she'd read enough descriptions of them to recognize them now. Their red-rimmed eyes, straggly, greasy hair, and loose, slobbery lips made them repulsive, but their smell was the most awful thing of all. It was so strong it attracted flies that buzzed around the trolls, landing on the corners of their eyes, on their mouths, and on the skin exposed through their raggedy clothes.

While Tomas and his men caught up, Aislin held her breath, watching as the trolls tossed Twinket back and forth. Poppy was there, flying after the doll, too small to do anything but scream at the trolls to stop.

The men reached the princess, gathering around to protect her. She was too stunned to speak, until one of the trolls ripped Twinket's arm off, tossing it into a tree where it lodged in the branches. At the sight of the poor, sobbing doll, Aislin screamed, "No!" even louder than Poppy. The trolls turned, wide grins splitting their scarred faces at the sight of new victims.

The men had already drawn their weapons and were taking aim at the shambling trolls when Tomas pushed Aislin behind him. From everything she had read, men and their meager weapons were no match for a troll, let alone seven. She was looking for bare rock when the manticore arrived, crashing through the underbrush, while the griffin dove from the sky to rake the trolls with his eagle talons.

The trolls bellowed, swatting at the griffin and throwing boulders, logs, and anything else they could pick up at the trumpeting manticore. Nimble and fleet of foot, the manticore avoided everything easily. When the troll holding Twinket threw her as well, Poppy swooped down, turning big in midair, just in time to grab the doll. The fairy tucked in her legs and arms when she landed, rolling across the forest floor with her body wrapped around Twinket.

"Over here!" Aislin called, even as she backed away from the trolls.

"My arm!" screamed Twinket, waving her remaining hand at the tree where her arm was barely visible.

"Here, take her!" Poppy cried, shoving the doll into Aislin's hands.

The fairy turned small again and darted to the tree. Too tiny to carry the arm, Poppy grabbed hold of it, tugged it loose, and hurled it as hard as she could at Aislin. Marden snatched it from the air and handed it to the princess, shaking his head when he saw that it was nothing more than fabric.

"Run!" Aislin shouted, and they retreated toward the road.

The trolls followed them, roaring and knocking down the smaller trees that stood in their way. The men paused now and then to shoot bolts from their crossbows, but the trolls paid the bolts no more attention than they did the flies that swarmed around them. When even the griffin and the manticore were unable to turn the trolls aside, Aislin began to fear that they might not reach the road and the narrow band of sunlight in time. As far as she could remember from her reading, sunlight was the only thing that trolls feared, because it could turn them to stone. Her party would be safe only if they could get to the other side.

She could hear the trolls drawing closer behind them when an idea occurred to her. Not knowing much more about trolls, she had no idea if it would do anything, but if it had worked with ogres...

Although singing wasn't easy when she was running, Aislin gave it everything she could. She sang the first song that popped into her head, a fairy drinking song that ended with everyone asleep in a meadow far from their homes. It was one of the ogres' favorites, and when she heard the trolls growing quiet behind her, she decided that it was now one of her favorite songs as well.

"Did you see that?" Cadby exclaimed as they finally reached the road. "As soon as the princess started to sing, the trolls stopped running and fell to the ground! I never would have believed it if I hadn't looked back and seen it myself."

"Just like ogres!" said Twinket.

"Except ogres don't fall down," Poppy reminded her.

"Aislin, are you going to introduce us?" Tomas asked, glancing at the fairy and the doll that could move and talk.

Thinking that it was too late for some secrets, Aislin turned to him and smiled. "Of course! These are Poppy and Twinket. They're my best friends and I've known them all my life."

"Uh, you're a fairy, right?" Tomas said to Poppy. "I saw you turn tiny and fly and everything. But what exactly is Twinket?"

"I'm a living doll!" Twinket explained.

"That's exactly right!" Aislin said with a laugh. "I couldn't have said it better!"

Twinket grinned, but a tear in her cheek made it look lopsided.

"Aislin, let me have Twinket for a minute," said Poppy. "I need to fix a few things."

Everyone kept walking as Poppy used her magic to reattach the doll's arm and mend the bigger holes. Tomas and his men watched, amazed, as the torn pieces drew back together and looked as good as new.

"Will you look at that!" Cadby breathed, regarding Poppy with respect. "A doll that can walk and talk and a fairy with real magic! You'd be mighty handy to have around on mending day! My old mother would be crazy about you!"

Poppy gave him a shy smile, her cheeks turning bright pink when he matched his pace to hers. Aislin had to grin when she saw the look on her friend's face.

"Why didn't you use your magic to stop the trolls?" asked Marden.

"Because fairy magic doesn't work on trolls," Poppy replied.

"Someone's magic does," Tomas said, giving Aislin a speculative look.

The griffin and the manticore came out of the forest and started to follow the group down the road. It made the men nervous, even though the beasts had just fought the trolls beside them. When the men put their hands on their weapons, Aislin dropped back to talk to the manticore. "Thank you for your help, but why were you following us?" she asked him.

"We said we'd do your bidding and we can't do that if we can't hear you. Besides, there's no reason to stay behind. We're supposed to protect Baibre," the griffin replied. "We don't sense her in her home now. She's with you. We talked it over and decided that we should follow you as long as you have her."

Aislin nodded. She could sense the magic in creatures around her; who was she to argue when others could sense such things as well?

"All right," she said. "You may stay with us as long as we're in the forest. But remember—you aren't to eat humans anymore."

"We already promised that we wouldn't!" the manticore blared, looking affronted.

"You're right, you did," said the princess, and she turned to rejoin the group.

When Aislin caught up with Poppy and Twinket, she asked, "What were you two doing here? I thought you were still in the castle."

"We were looking for you, of course," said Poppy. "As soon as I heard about the troops in the city, I grabbed Twinket and ran. We listened to talk in the street and heard which way your carriage went and followed it. I had a feeling we were getting close, but then those troll oafs grabbed Twinket and I didn't know what to do. I'm so glad you showed up when you did!"

"So am I!" Aislin said, and gave her friends each a hug.

They walked for more than an hour without seeing anyone or anything unusual. Marden finally told them that they had to turn west, and they left the road to head back through the forest. The griffin and the manticore had been trailing behind them, but they took the lead now, finding the way around thick underbrush and across a deep ravine.

They were passing through a forest glade when something darted past Tomas, only inches from his face. "What was that?" he cried, taking a step back.

Something tweaked Marden's nose while something else knocked Cadby's cap from his head and pulled his hair. Whatever was doing it was moving too fast for them to see.

"Stay here," Aislin told the human men as Poppy started to chase a tiny, moving target. When one flew close enough, Poppy's hand shot out and caught it. Aislin hurried to join her.

"Let me go!" cried a small, shrill voice.

Poppy opened her hand, revealing a tiny fairy dressed in fern tips. "They're angry flower fairies," Poppy told Aislin. "We must be in their meadow."

The fairy darted out of Poppy's hand and flew backward to get a better look at her. "You're a fairy, too!" she cried. "Where did you come from?"

"That's not possible!" cried a second fairy as they all came for a closer look. They were moving so quickly that it was hard to count how many were there.

"Who are you?" asked another.

"My name is Poppy," she said. "And this is Princess Aislin, granddaughter of Queen Surinen."

The fairies gasped. Some of them stopped beating their wings and almost dropped to the ground before they remembered to fly again. Others bumped into each other, looking confused, while some clapped their hands and looked at Aislin with joy in their eyes.

"Is the queen back?" one asked. "We've been waiting for this day for so long!"

"No," said Aislin. "She's not. Poppy and I are the only ones."

"Wait!" cried a fairy dressed in pink petals. "How do we know she really is who she says she is?"

"I'll show you," Aislin said, and held out her hand.

"I'm not touching her!" cried the fairy dressed in pink. "I don't trust her. You do it, Bluebell."

"Chicken!" cried the fairy wearing a bluebell cap. She darted over to land on Aislin's finger.

Aislin didn't move, but the contact was enough to make the fairy jump in surprise. "It's her!" she cried, and started dancing in midair. "It's her! It's her! It's really her!"

"A fairy princess?" said the one in pink. "But you aren't just fairy, are you? You aren't shaped like a fairy and your eyes are different."

Aislin shook her head. "I'm also a pedrasi princess. My father is King Carrigan, son of King Darinar and Queen Surinen. My mother is Queen Maylin, daughter of King Talus and Queen Amethyst."

"Wow! A lot has happened since we were left behind," Bluebell declared.

"I can't believe we couldn't tell that she was part fairy!" cried another fairy.

"Why is that hard to believe?" the fairy in pink asked. "We can't switch any more either."

"What do you mean?" Poppy asked her.

The fairy sighed. "After we were left behind—"

"It was our fault!" said Bluebell. "We slept in after a big party the night before and didn't wake up until everyone else was gone. We looked and looked, but couldn't find anyone, so we came back here. When word got out that the king and queen were gone, humans started hunting for fairies, so we stayed small and hid here so long that we've forgotten how to get big again. Without the king and queen here, there isn't as much magic around as there used to be. But you're back now and everything is going to be all right again!"

When Bluebell started dancing around Aislin, the others joined in, forming a flying garland of brightly clothed fairies that wove in and out around the princess. Suddenly Bluebell stopped and darted toward Aislin's face. "I know you said that you're the only one here now, but the others are coming back, aren't they? We need the king and queen. Nothing is the same as it used to be."

"I really don't know," Aislin told her.

"Please, please, please ask them to come back!" cried the fairy in pink.

"I'll tell them how much you need them," Aislin replied. "I promise."

Aislin and Poppy joined Tomas again. "What did you talk about?" he asked.

"All sorts of things," Aislin replied. "I just made

some new friends and a promise that I'll keep as soon as I can."

"And?" he prompted.

"And it's time to get going, don't you think?" she said with a smile.

Tomas grumbled, but she had no intention of sharing her conversation with the fairies.

The fairies seemed delighted with her promise. They escorted Aislin and her companions all the way to the edge of the forest, hanging back with Poppy while they asked about life in the fairy court and inquired after friends they hadn't seen in hundreds of years. Poppy told them that she'd come back to teach them how to get big again, which made them so happy that they started another dance. Aislin felt bad about leaving them behind, but even worse when she thought about how disappointed they'd be if her grandparents didn't bring all the other fairies back.

As she walked, she realized she was contemplating her family's return, something she never would have considered when she lived in Eliasind. That was their home, and had been for her entire life, but they'd had a home here before, and friends and family who missed them dearly. She had so much to discuss with her grandparents! Before she went back, however, she had to find out what the fairies were doing in the wider world beyond the forest.

The edge of the forest wasn't far from the border between Morain and Scarmander. The griffin and the manticore were reluctant to remain behind, but Aislin was firm and wouldn't let them leave the concealment of the forest. Avoiding the road and possible guards, Tomas led the group through fields and orchards, crossing the border on the way. They spent the night just beyond the border in a farmer's barn.

Even though Aislin was exhausted, her mind was roiling with too many things for her to fall asleep. King Tyburr knew about fairies. Clearly, the ceremony for the baby princess wasn't the first time he had summoned Morning Glory for a christening gift. That meant that he had known about fairies before he ever visited Eliasind. Was it possible that he knew that fairies lived in the land between the mountains before the visit? Did he know that fairies lived in her parents' castle when he was there? How did he find out about the pass, anyway? And even with the pass open, it wasn't easy to get through and would have been hard to find—unless someone had told him where to look. He wanted to go back, too. Was he just looking for a way into

Scarmander like Poppy seemed to think, or was he looking for something else?

Before Aislin fell asleep, she decided that she would very much like to have a conversation with Morning Glory, the fairy who had visited King Tyburr's court and the only fairy that she knew had traveled between the human kingdoms. Maybe she would have some answers.

Chapter 17

IT WAS A LOT easier to sneak out of Morain undetected than it was to slip into Scarmander. When they woke the next morning, they found the duke's troops surrounding the barn. The officers were suspicious until Tomas came out of the barn with his hands up, yawning and bleary-eyed. They greeted him warmly, escorting Tomas, Aislin, and Poppy to a carriage that whisked them to the capital.

The carriage was carrying them up a busy, winding road to the castle on top of a hill when Aislin turned to Tomas and said, "Can you arrange for me to meet Morning Glory? It's very important that I talk to her without alerting her ahead of time."

"The only time she comes to the city is when a

wealthy noble summons her for a christening gift," said Tomas. "I suppose I can see if anyone is planning a christening."

"Fine, as long as I can see her soon," said Aislin. "I want to speak with her before I meet Aghamonda, and I have a feeling that could happen at any time."

"I'll see what I can do," Tomas replied. "Look over there! That's my favorite tailor shop. And that's where they sell the freshest peaches from a farm just outside the city."

Aislin enjoyed seeing the sights with Tomas, but she enjoyed his enthusiasm even more. The Tomas she'd known back in King Tyburr's castle had been quiet and subdued. She had a feeling that she was seeing the real Tomas now.

When they reached the castle, the steward escorted Aislin and Poppy up a flight of stairs to one of the most beautiful suites of rooms they had ever seen. Decorated in blues and greens, it was the same shades as Aislin's favorite lake near Fairengar, where nymphs played in the water and the fish were so tame that they'd take crusts from her hand. The two girls walked from room to room, and Aislin had to squeeze Twinket more than once when the doll wiggled, wanting to get down and run around.

"Not yet," Aislin whispered, so the steward wouldn't hear her.

When they had seen all three rooms, the steward led them to a large window that looked out over the city and the bay. He pointed to the ocean beyond, which made Poppy gasp and lean so far out that Aislin was afraid she would fall.

"I'll have water brought up so you may bathe," the steward said, not even glancing at Aislin's clothes made filthy from her travels.

"Thank you," Aislin told him, grateful for his thoughtfulness.

The moment they were alone, Aislin set Twinket on the floor and joined Poppy at the window. They were still watching the big ships sail in and out of the bay when there was a knock on the door.

"Twinket!" Poppy said, and the doll collapsed on the floor.

The fairy went to the door and peeked out, then stepped back, opening it wider as a group of servants brought in a tub, towels, scented soap, and bucket after bucket of hot water. As they left, another maid brought in gowns and laid them out on the bed.

"So you may select a gown to wear to meet King

Ozwalt, Your Highness," the maid told Aislin. "Would you like me to stay to help you bathe?"

Aislin hadn't had anyone help her bathe since she was a toddler, and she wasn't about to ask for help now. "My servant will assist me," Aislin told the young woman. "Thank you for offering."

The maid smiled and curtsied, closing the door behind her.

"You want me to help?" Poppy asked, surprised.

"No, I want you to leave the room so I can take off this gown and get in that tub," Aislin told her, already fumbling with the buttons.

"I mean, I could stay and scrub your back if you want me to," Poppy said, her smile getting broader.

"Get...out...now!" Aislin ordered her friend, her grin just as big.

Poppy was laughing as she left the room, but by then Aislin had her gown half over her head. She was about to start on her undergarments when she felt the chain still around her neck. Although she had guarded it easily enough on her way to Scarmander, she had a feeling that it would no longer be safe with her—not when she was sure she was going to meet Aghamonda and had no idea when the meeting would take place.

Pulling the chain over her head, she looked around, trying to decide where she could hide it. When Aislin glanced toward the window and saw the doll perched on the ledge, she knew just what to do.

"Twinket, would you come here please?" she asked the doll.

Twinket turned and gave her a saucy look. "What, you want *me* to scrub your back?" she asked.

Aislin shook her head, no longer in a joking mood. "No, I want you to do something very important. Here, take this." She waited until the doll had scrambled off the ledge and run over to the tub. "I want you to put it somewhere very safe. Don't let anyone know where it is, and that goes for Poppy and me. Keep it safe until I ask for it back."

Twinket took the locket from her and examined it closely. "Ooh," she said. "No one has ever asked me to do something this important before. I'll guard it with my life, I promise! Just tell me one thing— what is it?"

"An important piece of jewelry that I'm holding onto for someone," Aislin replied. "A bad person wants it, and we can't let her have it."

"Then I'll keep it extra safe," the doll declared, and began to look around the room.

"Don't hide it in here," Aislin told her. "I don't want to see where you put it."

"All right," Twinket said, and ran to the not-quite-closed door.

"I hope I'm doing the right thing," Aislin murmured as she watched the door shut.

Aislin was ready by the time Tomas came to take her to meet the king. Bathed, dressed in a gown of pale lavender silk, and with her hair held back with pearl-headed pins, she was the image of a beautiful princess.

"You look lovely!" Tomas said when she came to the door.

"Thank you," she said, her cheeks turning pink.

"You don't need to worry," Tomas told her as she set her hand on his arm. "My father and King Ozwalt are going to be crazy about you."

"I'm not worried," she said. *Not about that, at least,* she thought. Making a good impression on humans didn't concern her. Finding out why Aghamonda wanted her sister caught in amber did. Ever since she'd given the locket to Twinket, she couldn't stop thinking about the fairy sisters. Why would any fairy want to trap a member of her own family? Could she be trying to keep her safe? But then, why the subterfuge? No matter how she turned the idea of a fairy caught in amber around in her head, she couldn't think of a good reason that made any sense. Unfortunately, some very bad ones did.

As they approached the throne room, a page bowed and opened the door for them. Tomas patted her hand where it rested on his other arm, as if to reassure her. Aislin thought it was sweet, but he needn't have worried. She was used to the throne room at Fairengar that was far grander and more impressive than anything in the human lands. Even her fairy grandparents, who could make the fiercest warrior tremble, had never intimidated her. She had played at their feet while they held court too many times when she was little, and knew better than to let courtiers' haughty manners and snobbish looks bother her. If anyone could look impressive, it was a member of the royal fairy family.

Aislin looked around as they walked down the center of the long, narrow throne room, noting the crowd that had gathered to see the new arrival. They were all dressed in their finest and smiled when she glanced in their direction. Some of the smiles were genuine, while others were obviously phony.

Windows high on the walls let in enough sunlight to make torches and candles unnecessary during the day. Below the windows, tapestries depicting the sea and its creatures lined the walls. She was delighted to see that the stone floor was laid in bands of light and dark to resemble row after row of waves. In a fairy castle, the waves would have appeared to move. Here they were stationary, but almost as delightful.

As Tomas escorted Aislin down the length of the room, her gaze traveled to the gilded throne. An elderly man wearing a crown occupied the throne, while a big man with dark hair like Tomas's stood by his side. The big man's back was straight and his head was held high as if he was the king, rather than the seated man whose back was bent with age. Aislin assumed that the dark-haired man was the Duke of Isely, Tomas's father. The closer Aislin and Tomas drew, the more she could see how frail the old man looked. His eyes were rheumy, the blue of his irises faded. His hands shook when he gestured to her.

Tomas led Aislin to the foot of the dais before saying, "Your Majesty, may I present Her Royal Highness Princess Aislin."

Stepping away from Tomas, Aislin curtsied almost as deeply as she would have to her grandparents. She waited while the king murmured something too faint to hear.

"Please rise, Your Highness," said the duke. "On behalf of His Majesty King Ozwalt and myself, welcome to Scarmander. May your stay here be a pleasant one."

King Ozwalt nodded and smiled, but his expression was vague and his gaze soon wandered. The duke smiled as well; there was nothing vague about his expression when he gave his son an approving nod. Aislin had a feeling that she had just passed some sort of test. Tomas took her hand again and led her from the throne room.

"Now *that* is how a princess is supposed to be welcomed, unlike the way they handled your arrival in Morain!" he said as they entered the corridor. "I have good news for you. I made some inquiries and learned that the wife of a not-so-rich noble has recently given him an heir. The christening is scheduled in five days' time."

"That isn't soon enough!" Aislin began.

Tomas held up his hand. "I already met with the noble. He can't afford a fairy christening gift, but when I said that I would give him sufficient gold coins as my gift to his son, he was happy to change the date and invite us both. I didn't tell him who I was bringing, just that there would be two of us. The ceremony is going to be held tomorrow. Why is it so important that you speak with Morning Glory?"

"If I'm right, she can answer some very important questions," Aislin replied.

"Oh, I meant to tell you, we won't be seeing Rory while he's here," said Tomas. "It seems that he tried to escape into the city his very first day in the castle. Now he's locked in his chambers under guard. He talks constantly, and the guards find him really annoying. He never has known how to be nice to people."

"I'm glad we won't be seeing him," Aislin replied. "I think we both had more than enough of Rory in Morain."

Chapter 18

THE CHRISTENING WAS HELD in the noble couple's mansion just inside the city wall. Built from pale gray stone streaked with pink, it was positioned on the hillside so that its large windows looked out over the bay far below. Tomas and Aislin were the last of the guests to arrive. The noble and his wife met them at the door and were effusive in their greetings. Aislin didn't want a fuss made over her, so Tomas introduced her as his friend. Even that brought her more attention than she wanted.

When the guests gathered in a large room fronting the bay, Aislin stayed in the back near the door. She watched the ceremony, waiting for the fairy's arrival. As soon as Morning Glory entered the room, Aislin slipped out and listened from the hallway. Even without seeing what was happening, she could hear when the noble paid Morning Glory and the fairy gave the gift to the infant. When Morning Glory stepped out of the room, Aislin was ready for her. Before the fairy had spotted her, the princess stepped up and took hold of her arm.

"Come with me," Aislin said as she drew the fairy into a side room.

Morning Glory was too confused to try to get away.

"You need to answer my questions," said Aislin. "How well do you know Aghamonda?"

"You're a fairy with royal blood!" Morning Glory cried. "I can feel it. What are you doing here?"

Aislin sighed. "I'm here to ask you questions. How well do you know Aghamonda?"

"What if I don't want to answer you?" Morning Glory asked.

Drawing power from the stone beneath her feet, Aislin projected it into her voice. "I'm someone you don't want to fool with," she told her.

Morning Glory gasped and tried to pull her hand back, but Aislin wouldn't let go. "I'll ask you one more time—how well do you know Aghamonda?"

Morning Glory licked her lips. "Not well at all," she replied.

"You're lying," said Aislin. "Try again."

This time she let a hint of power trickle through her hand, giving the fairy a tiny shock. Aislin had never done that before, but she wasn't beyond experimenting when she needed to. It made the fairy hiss as she drew in a breath. "I've met her a few times," said Morning Glory, her eyes fixed on a point above Aislin's head.

"Another lie," Aislin told her.

This time the touch of power was so strong that it singed Morning Glory's sleeve and she yelped in pain. Aislin had yet to learn how to control the amount of power she let through.

"I work for her sometimes, all right?" said the fairy. "I can go just about anywhere because of the christenings. I see things, and I tell her about them. Sometimes I give messages to other people for her. That's all!"

"The truth, finally!" said Aislin. "Tell me, did you give a message to King Tyburr about a pass recently?"

"How did you hear about that? Unless..." Morning Glory looked at Aislin more closely. Suddenly her eyes widened and she tried to pull her hand free. "You're from the other side!" she cried. "That *is* where the fairies went!"

Aislin held on tightly. Another touch of power, less than the one that had singed her, and the fairy stopped struggling. "What did Aghamonda have you tell King Tyburr?" Aislin asked.

"Nothing much, really. Just the directions for a pass that was open to the land between the mountains. She wanted me to tell him that if he took it, he could find a secret way into Scarmander."

"And how did Aghamonda benefit from giving him this information?" asked Aislin.

"I don't know. I told her what he said, but it wasn't much," said Morning Glory. "I met with him after he came back. He said that he didn't find the pass into Scarmander. He had a dream that made him come home early, so he didn't go very far. He did say that a girl saved his life, and he brought her back with him because he couldn't leave her in a haunted castle where strange things happened. He said she was a princess. It was you, wasn't it?"

Aislin wasn't about to tell the fairy any more than necessary, but she still had a few questions to ask. "What did Aghamonda do when you told her what King Tyburr had said?"

Morning Glory shrugged. "She was disappointed that he didn't have more to say. She didn't mention it before I told him about the pass, but later she said things that made me think she'd expected him to find a lot of people there." She gasped and her eyes went wide again. "Do you think she suspected that the fairies went to the land between the mountains?"

"Has Aghamonda asked you to do or say anything else since you reported back to her?"

"No! We haven't spoken since then."

"Good," said Aislin. "I want you to promise me that you won't talk to her anymore. Go far away from here and don't let her know that we've spoken, or that you're leaving. I don't blame you for aligning yourself with Aghamonda; I know that fairies have had to do all sorts of things to survive. If you leave now, you'll be forgiven. However, if you help her again, you'll be considered a traitor to your kind. Do you understand me?"

Morning Glory nodded. "I do. I promise. I'll go right away. But tell me, you're related to Queen Surinen, aren't you? You have the same eyes."

"I am," Aislin whispered, and held her finger to her lips. "But you can't tell anyone."

"Oh, I won't!" said Morning Glory.

The moment Aislin released her, Morning Glory ran out the door, clutching the noble's payment to her chest. The fairy almost bumped into Tomas in the doorway.

"Did you learn anything from her?" he asked Aislin as Morning Glory darted off.

"Yes, but now I have more questions and I'm not sure how to find the answers."

When the princess returned to her chambers, Twinket was still sitting in the corner, exactly where she'd been that morning before Aislin left. After Aislin put on more comfortable clothes, she invited her friends to sit with her in front of the window to watch the ships in the harbor. Although Poppy joined her, Twinket stayed in the corner, saying, "I'm fine where I am."

"She hasn't moved all day," Poppy said. "I think there's something wrong with her."

Aislin shook her head. "I think she's fine. I gave her a job to do and she's taking it very seriously."

"What kind of job?" asked Poppy. "It can't be much if she can do it without moving."

"It's important. Perhaps the most important job she's ever taken on. Oh, look at the ship with the blue sails. Isn't that beautiful!" Aislin said, hoping to distract her friend.

The girls hadn't been sitting by the window for long when there was a knock on the door. It was Tomas with news for Aislin.

"Aghamonda is here," he said as Poppy shut the door, leaving them alone to talk. "She arrived this morning while we were at the christening. She's already taken over one of the towers from top to bottom. I don't know why Father puts up with her. Anyway, she summoned me to her tower as if she was a queen, then questioned me like I was some sort of criminal. I really don't like that fairy."

"What did she ask you?" said Aislin.

"She wanted to know if I gave Baibre the locket," Tomas replied. "When I said that I had, she asked where it was now. I played dumb and said that her sister had it, of course. She got mad and threw a glass bottle at the wall. It shattered and I left before she could throw something at me."

"She sounds like a delightful person," Aislin said.

"She's bound to be at supper tonight," Tomas told her. "We can skip eating in the Great Hall and have our food brought up here if you'd like."

"That's very tempting," said Aislin, "but I think it's time I met Aghamonda."

"That reminds me," Tomas continued. "I'd never

238

seen Aghamonda before, but now that I've met her and her sister I was wondering something. Why is it that, if they're twins, Aghamonda looks so much younger and prettier?"

"She's a fairy," Aislin said. "Fairies can let themselves age, or keep themselves looking young with a simple spell. Aghamonda may be incredibly old, but she's using magic to make herself look young."

"Huh," said Tomas. "Too bad she doesn't use her magic to make herself nicer."

Aislin wasn't sure if she should dress like a princess for supper, or wear a less flattering gown that wouldn't draw attention. She thought about it long and hard, finally deciding that she should dress the way she would normally. Aghamonda probably had a good idea who she was anyway, and no disguise was going to conceal Aislin's magic. Although she wasn't going to deliberately reveal who she was, she also wasn't going to hide it.

Aislin wore a beautiful cornflower-blue dress. As Tomas came to the door that evening, he whistled when he saw her. "You look fantastic!" he said, taking her arm. "All the ladies in the court are going to be jealous!"

"I wasn't thinking about the ladies of the court when I put this on," Aislin told him. "I just didn't want to look as if I was trying to hide who I was from Aghamonda."

Tomas snorted. "I don't care what that fairy thinks. If she bothers you, she'll have to deal with me!"

"That's very sweet," Aislin told him. "But let's not judge her just yet. I need to meet her and see what kind of fairy we're facing before I make any real decisions about her."

"I told you what she did this afternoon," said Tomas.

Aislin nodded. "I know, and that definitely counts against her."

When they reached the Great Hall, Aghamonda was already sitting beside the king, right where Aislin had been seated the night before. The fairy was dressed in brilliant red petals that made her impossible to ignore. "Oh, look," the fairy announced in a loud voice. "It's the princess that everyone is talking about! Come sit beside me. I want to get to know you."

"You don't have to sit there if you don't want to," Tomas whispered in Aislin's ear.

Aislin smiled and murmured, "I don't mind. This should be interesting."

When Aislin took the seat, Aghamonda beamed as if she'd already won some sort of contest. *It hasn't even begun yet,* Aislin said to herself, then turned and smiled at the fairy.

"So you're making the rounds of the kingdoms. Are you having fun?" the fairy asked her.

"Yes, I am," Aislin replied. "I hear you arrived at the castle today and have already made yourself at home in the tower. Are you here for a visit or have you moved in permanently?"

"Just a visit," the fairy said, her smile becoming brittle. "Is it true that you rescued King Tyburr from a horrible death?"

Aislin shrugged. "I stopped a bear from mauling him, if that's what you mean. The king was hunting in a place he should never have been."

"Oh, really? And why is that?" asked Aghamonda.

"Because someone who didn't have the right sent him there," Aislin said, deliberately misreading the question.

Aghamonda's eyes were glittering when she said, "I meant, why shouldn't he have been there?"

"It was closed off for a very good reason," replied Aislin as she reached for a ripe pear.

The fairy leaned close and said in a harsh whisper,

"Is that so? And what were the people left outside supposed to do?"

"Respect the reason that the people were inside, and know that they were never shut out intentionally," Aislin said in a normal voice.

King Ozwalt gestured to the eel stew that a server was offering the fairy. "Try some of the stew! It's my favorite," he said in his wavering voice.

"Not now!" Aghamonda snapped.

The king shrugged and reached for his spoon.

"Why *are* you here?" Aghamonda asked Aislin.

"Because Tomas is my friend and he invited me," Aislin said, and turned to give Tomas a sweet smile. She turned back when he nearly choked on his bite of eel.

"Uh-huh," the fairy said, sounding doubtful.

"And why are you here?" Aislin asked her.

"Perhaps you'd like the roast duck?" the king said as a serving maid presented the next dish.

Aghamonda made a disgusted face and said, "No, thank you."

"Fairies don't eat meat, Your Majesty," Aislin told him.

"Then why aren't you eating it?" Aghamonda asked, looking Aislin up and down. "You're no fairy."

242

"And you're very rude," Aislin said, and helped herself from a bowl of parsnips. "You didn't answer my question. Why are you here?"

"I came to help King Ozwalt fight a war," Aghamonda replied.

Suddenly Aislin went cold. "What do you mean?" she asked the fairy. "What do you plan to do?"

"Whatever it takes," Aghamonda said, and turned to face the king. "Isn't that right, Your Majesty?"

When the fairy continued to talk to the king with her back to Aislin, the princess knew that she wasn't going to get any more out of her. Turning to Tomas, Aislin said, "We can leave whenever you're ready. I'm finished here and I have a lot of thinking to do."

Chapter 19

"DID YOU HEAR WHAT Aghamonda said?" Aislin asked as she and Tomas walked down the corridor. "She's here to help King Ozwalt with the war."

"I heard," Tomas replied. "My father told me about it this afternoon. He thinks that having her on our side will make all the difference."

"It will make a difference, all right, but I don't know if it will be good or bad. Your father and the king shouldn't trust her. She's up to something and I have a feeling that the only one who will benefit is Aghamonda."

Aislin wanted to tell him more, but that would mean revealing things she wasn't free to share. Aghamonda had already tried to help King Tyburr by telling him about the back way into Scarmander through the land between the mountains. Even though King Tyburr hadn't located the route, the fairy had done something that could have turned the war in his favor. And now she was here saying that she wanted to help King Ozwalt. She was playing the two sides against each other, which was wrong. What was even worse was that she was involving herself in the war at all. Keeping fairies out of human conflicts was the very reason that the fairy king and queen had left the human lands. Aislin's grandparents were going to be furious when they heard about it, and they were bound to want to stop her. In the meantime, Aislin had to do something.

After saying goodbye to Tomas, Aislin returned to her chambers to think. "What's wrong?" Poppy asked the minute the princess walked in the door. "Something happened; I can see it on your face."

"Aghamonda says she's here to help King Ozwalt, but she already tried to help King Tyburr. I need to convince Tomas's father not to trust her, except I can't without some sort of proof of what she's doing."

Poppy sounded eager. "Do you want me to spy on her? I'm very good at it now."

"I don't know," said Aislin. "This wouldn't be like

spying on King Tyburr. Aghamonda is a fairy and has the power to do something nasty."

"Don't worry about me! I'm a fairy, too," Poppy replied. "She'll never even know I'm there."

Aislin shook her head. "I really don't think you should. It wouldn't be safe."

"What about contacting your family?" asked Poppy. "I think they should know what's going on."

"Not yet," said Aislin. "Not until we learn more about Aghamonda's plans."

Although Poppy didn't seem happy, she didn't mention her spying mission or contacting the fairy royals again that evening. When Aislin went to bed, she was sure she'd lie awake, tossing and turning, but she fell asleep right away.

She woke in the morning, certain that something was wrong. Throwing back the covers, she jumped out of bed and ran to the next room. To her relief, Twinket was just where she'd been the day before.

"Poppy's gone," Twinket told her. "She left last night and hasn't come back."

"She went out without telling me?" said Aislin. "Where did she go?"

"To spy on Aghamonda," Twinket said. "She wanted me to go with her, but I already have a job to do."

"What time did she leave?"

"About an hour after you went to bed. She wanted to have the proof you needed when you got up this morning."

"I have to go find her!" Aislin cried. "Aghamonda better not have hurt her!"

Aislin hurried to her room to get dressed. She was slipping on her shoes when there was a knock on the door. Although she knew Poppy wouldn't knock, she was still hoping it was her friend when she ran to answer it.

"Hi!" Tomas said. "Want to have breakfast with me?"

Aislin shook her head. "I can't eat now. I have to find Poppy."

"She isn't here?" Tomas asked, looking around the room.

"She went to spy on Aghamonda," Twinket announced from the corner. "Aislin needs proof that Aghamonda is helping both sides so you can show it to your father."

"Twinket!" exclaimed Aislin. "You weren't supposed to tell him that!"

"Why not? It's the truth, isn't it?" said the doll. "And he is on our side."

"If you're going to the tower, I'll go with you," Tomas told Aislin. "I know my way around there and you don't. I just saw Aghamonda heading to the Great Hall, so if we're going, we should go now. If she comes back and finds us in the tower, I can always say that I left something there before she took it over."

"I'm ready if you are," said Aislin.

It took them only a few minutes to reach the tower. Tomas tried the door and found it unlocked.

"I don't like this," said Aislin. "Why would she leave the door unlocked?"

"Maybe she's forgetful," Tomas told her. "Or maybe she assumes that no one would bother a powerful fairy's belongings."

"Or maybe she's inside waiting for someone to come in, like a spider waiting for a fly," said Aislin.

"Or there's that," said Tomas. "Don't worry, she won't hurt us. She's in my great-uncle's castle and she couldn't get away with it."

"I doubt she'd care about that," Aislin said as she followed Tomas into the first-floor room. "I don't think she's the kind of fairy to let much get in her way."

They started looking for Poppy, calling her name as they went from floor to floor and room to room. They were on the third floor when Aislin noticed a map spread open on a table. The map showed all of Morain, with a mark on the Galiman River. Another map lay rolled into a tube beside it. When Tomas unrolled it, they found that it was a map of Scarmander.

Aislin spread out a third map. She gasped when she saw that it was a very, very old map of the land between the mountains. "I wonder where she got this," she murmured.

"Got what?" asked Tomas, coming over to look.

Aislin let it roll up again. "Just an old map," she said.

"Here's another one," said Tomas. "It's in a tube."

Aislin leaned closer as he pulled the end off the tube. A gray mist washed out, enveloping them. Moments later, they lay on the floor, unconscious.

When she woke up, Aislin couldn't see a thing. Everything was black, and it took her a moment to realize that she was somewhere with absolutely no light. Because she was half pedrasi, she could see in very little light, but she was as blind as anyone else in the complete dark. The air was cold, too, and the surface under her felt like stone. Reaching out with her mind, she discovered that she was underground with stone all around her. Her pedrasi abilities enabled her to see where the stone was and where it wasn't even when she couldn't see with her eyes. She could actually tell lots of things—what kind of rock it was, how deep it went, and where passages cut through it.

Aislin turned her head when she heard the trickle of water dripping slowly down the wall behind her. Casting around with her mind again, she located the tiniest fracture that allowed the water to escape. Apparently, the rock was filled with tiny fault lines.

Aislin sat up. She was mad at herself for not having contacted her relatives the night before. Putting things off was rarely a good idea. Lying around now wasn't going to help either. "Hello! Is anyone there?" she called.

Poppy's voice sounded small and far away. "I'm over here! I was looking around the tower and I heard Aghamonda coming, so I got small and hid. She found me anyway and froze me so I couldn't move. The next thing I knew, she'd stuck me in a jar! I've tried and tried, but I can't open it. I think she used some special magic to keep me in."

"Are you all right?" Aislin called back.

"Would you be all right if you were in a jar?" the fairy said, sounding grumpy. "I'm not hurt, if that's what you mean."

"Where are we?" asked Aislin.

"In the dungeon under her tower. She caught me before I'd barely started snooping and brought me down here. I must have been here for days and days."

"How long have I been here?" Aislin asked her.

"A couple of hours," said the fairy.

"Then you haven't been here all that long. Is Tomas here?"

"He's in the cell next to yours. He's still asleep."

A tiny speck of light pierced the dark. Suddenly Aislin could see. "Shh! There's a light. Someone's coming."

It was Aghamonda, carrying a torch as she came toward them down a tunnel. Aislin hurriedly looked around. The stone walls had distinctive striations in them and looked rough and unfinished. Other cells lined the walls of an open space; Tomas was in the one next to Aislin's, lying on his side. The space itself was empty except for an old wooden table. A glass jar rested on the table. When Aislin noticed something move inside the jar, she knew she'd found Poppy.

Aghamonda came closer and saw Aislin standing

in her cell. "You're awake, I see. I wondered how long you'd be out. I've been trying some new magic and I wasn't sure how well it would work. It should prove useful against Tyburr's troops."

Aghamonda glanced at Tomas who was just beginning to stir. Turning to the table, she picked up Poppy's jar and shook it. After a particularly hard shake, Poppy cried out. Aghamonda laughed and set the jar back on the table.

"I'm leaving now," she announced. "It's time I used a little magic to help Ozwalt in the war. The Duke of Isely and his troops set out in the middle of the night. He thinks he's in charge, but he's about to learn just how little control he really has. I'm not sure when I'll be back. It could be a few hours, or a few days, or I might forget that you're down here entirely. No one knows you're here. No one will hear you call for help. You'll never be able to get out on your own. Goodbye! Have fun!"

Aghamonda took the torch when she left. The darkness seemed even more complete with the torch gone.

"Don't worry, Aislin," Tomas called from the next cell. "I'll figure something out!"

Aislin wasn't about to wait for someone else to help her. Closing her eyes, she centered herself and read the rock. Her magic allowed her to feel where it was strongest and weakest. She could feel the cracks and the fissures and how much pressure each could withstand. Reaching deep into the rock, she pulled strength from it, then touched the rock near the door and sent the power back into the fracture lines, a touch here, a little more there, breaking the rock a bit at a time.

At the sound of grating and cracking rock, Tomas cried out. Aislin was careful, though, shoring it up here, strengthening it there, so that the cracks didn't run too far or go where she didn't want them. She didn't open her eyes again until the door to her cell fell to the ground with a crash.

"What just happened?" Tomas cried. "Aislin, are you all right?"

"I'm fine," she replied as she stepped over the door, feeling her way out of the cell with her mind and her hands. Getting herself out in the dark was one thing, but she didn't want to frighten Tomas.

"Poppy, could you please flutter your wings?" Aislin asked her friend.

"I'm still in a jar, you know. I can't go anywhere," said the fairy.

"I don't need you to go anywhere. I just need some light."

"Oh, right!" Poppy exclaimed. A moment later a speck of light appeared in the jar as the fairy fluttered her wings. The faster she moved them, the brighter the light became. It grew until the jar seemed to be filled with it.

"Aislin, how did you get out?" Tomas asked when he saw her standing by the table.

"I told you that I'm half pedrasi, remember?" she replied. "Fairies get all the attention, but you'd be surprised what pedrasi can do."

"You did that yourself?" he asked, astonishment plain on his face when he saw the cell door lying on the ground.

"Yes," she replied, "and I'm not finished yet."

Poppy's wings faltered as Aislin began to untie the string that held a scrap of leather on top. When the way was clear, the little fairy zipped out of the jar and flew around her friend three times. By then Aislin was already on her way to Tomas's cell.

"Stand back," she told him. Once he had moved to the back of the cell, she set her hand beside the door,

254

closed her eyes, and "felt" for tiny cracks in the rock. His door fell off even faster than her own.

"You did that?" he said, his eyes wide. "That was amazing! How did you do it?"

"I can't do a lot of things that a fairy can do, but I can do all that a pedrasi can, plus a few things that I think are all my own," said Aislin. "Come on, let's get out of here. Like Aghamonda said, there's no telling when she'll be back."

With Poppy flying ahead to light the way, they were soon climbing the stairs to the next level. The fairy turned big again when Aislin opened the door letting the sunlight in.

"I need to find out if my father actually left," Tomas told them. "I don't think we can believe anything that Aghamonda says, but if he's gone, I want to find out where he's headed."

A trumpet sounded high and clear; Aislin looked puzzled as she said, "That's not possible."

"Is that the manticore?" asked Tomas. "He sounds a lot better now."

Aislin shook her head. "That's no manticore! Those are my grandfather's warriors announcing that he's here. The fairy king has come to Scarmander! How did he know where to find me?"

"I called an eagle and sent her with a message before I went to search Aghamonda's tower," said Poppy. "I know you wanted to wait, but I thought we'd already waited long enough!"

Chapter 20

AISLIN AND POPPY RACED out of the tower and through the castle, barely noting that it seemed emptier than usual. Aghamonda had been right about one thing— the troops had already gone. The people that were left were running around, shouting about barring the doors, but the princess tore past them with Poppy on her heels. Aislin was breathless when she finally reached the hall that led to the courtyard.

"Open that door!" she ordered the men trying to lift the heavy wooden bar in place. "That's not your enemy out there. That's my grandfather!"

Some of the men turned to her, bewildered, but the rest continued to struggle with the bar. Aislin pushed past them. Drawing strength from the stone floor, she flipped the bar on its end with one touch. People gasped as she flung the door open and started toward the steps.

Her fairy grandfather was there, dressed in shining white. The light reflecting off his armor and that of the knights accompanying him was nearly blinding. Aislin paused on the top step and squinted. Her father was there as well.

Aislin cried out and ran down the steps as her father and grandfather dismounted. Her father reached her first and picked her up. "Are you all right?" he asked. "We were so worried about you, especially after that falcon brought the message mentioning King Tyburr's plans. I was lucky to be at the castle when Poppy's eagle arrived with her message. I think that lucky charm you gave me did its job."

"I'm fine," Aislin said as her father set her down. "But—"

Her fairy grandfather pulled her into his arms and squeezed her so tightly that Aislin squeaked. "Here's our girl!" he said. "We rode all the way here at a gallop. The message didn't tell us much. What's going on?"

"There's a fairy named Aghamonda," she said as soon as she could breathe again. "She's gone off to help King Ozwalt's army."

"What?" roared King Darinar.

"She's playing two human armies against each other," Aislin told him. "Aghamonda is the one who sent word to King Tyburr about the pass into Eliasind."

"Where is she now?" asked King Darinar.

"I can answer that," Tomas said from the top of the stairs. "My father was taking his army to Galiman River crossing. My great-uncle just told me the whole thing."

"This is my friend Tomas," said Aislin. "His father is the Duke of Isely, and his great-uncle is King Ozwalt. Tomas was helping me find out what we could about Aghamonda when she knocked us out and locked us in cells."

"I see," said King Darinar. "What else can you tell us about this fairy?"

"She trapped her sister in an amber necklace," Tomas told him. "But we don't know why."

"They were both left behind when the fairies moved away," said Aislin. "From what I've learned, her sister, Baibre, hid in the forest, but Aghamonda kept in touch with humans because she wanted to influence their affairs. I can show you the tower where she keeps her things if that would help."

"It might," said the fairy king.

"I'm going to the rooms to change my clothes," Poppy whispered to Aislin. "I smell like whatever dead thing Aghamonda kept in that jar last."

Poppy was running off when the fairy king turned to survey the courtyard. "I can tell a powerful fairy was here. I can feel her magic. We go this way, if I'm not mistaken."

Aislin's grandfather took the lead, heading directly toward the tower. The humans who hadn't run off to hide watched wide-eyed as fairy royalty strode through the Great Hall. Even without the sunlight playing on their armor, it glowed with a light of its own. The fairies didn't seem to notice a woman faint as they passed by.

Aislin followed them into the tower, then showed them the way to the table where the maps were still laid out. Both men looked angry when they saw the map of the land between the mountains. When Aislin caught a glimpse of her rumpled reflection in a mirror, she turned to the two fairy royals and said, "Do you mind if I get cleaned up while you look around?"

"Go ahead, child," said her grandfather. "But we won't be long."

Aislin hurried from the tower and ran straight to her chambers. She was so happy to see members of her family! Now that they were here, they could take care of Aghamonda and she could go home and everything would be all right again. She was nearly humming with happiness when she opened the door to her rooms and ran in, only to find Poppy looking distraught.

"What's wrong?" she asked her friend.

"I can't find Twinket!" the fairy told her. "She's not in the corner where she's been sitting and I've looked everywhere. I called and called, but she doesn't answer! Oh, Aislin, what could have happened to her?"

Aislin's heart skipped a beat. Twinket was missing? But Twinket was always there when she needed her. The little doll was as much a constant in Aislin's life as the sun and the moon. The only time they'd been apart for more than a few hours was when King Tyburr had sent Aislin away in the carriage, but even then she was certain Poppy was looking after her. Sure, what happened with the trolls had been terrible, but she'd known Poppy could fix the doll once they got her back. Twinket had never been missing before! While Poppy was Aislin's best friend, Twinket was more than that. It was like part of Aislin was gone.

Suddenly all the fear and hurt and sorrow that had been building up inside Aislin since the day King Tyburr took her from her home was more than she could bear. She could feel her heart racing and a lump forming in her throat. Tears pricked her eyes and she had trouble catching her breath.

Her father burst into the room, looking around frantically. "What's wrong?" he asked when he saw Aislin's face. "Your mother gave me your mood stone. Look at it!"

The stone was a cloudy gray—a color it had never been before.

"Twinket is gone," Poppy told him.

"Was she over here?" Aislin's grandfather asked, pointing to the corner of the room.

Aislin nodded. "That's where she spent the last day or so."

King Darinar bent down to examine the corner more closely. "Aghamonda left a magic trail from her tower to these rooms. The feeling is strongest here. She's probably the one who took your doll."

Aislin turned to the door. "Let's go find that fairy!"

"Don't you want to get cleaned up first?" asked her father.

"I don't want to do anything except go after Aghamonda," Aislin replied. "Nothing else matters now."

It was the first time Aislin had ridden a fairy horse. After the first few minutes of panic while she raced across the countryside, she decided that it had to be one of the most glorious things she'd ever experienced. It was no wonder that fairies loved the horses and talked about them all the time. She probably would too, now. It was unfortunate that Poppy's normally pink cheeks were ashen and that she clung to her horse as if it was about to buck her off at any moment. The fairy girl had never ridden a horse before, let alone a high-tempered fairy steed.

Aislin had convinced her father that it was only right to let Tomas come along, after all she had been through with the human boy. When Tomas heard that he could go with them, he couldn't stop smiling. He was thrilled to do anything with the fairies, and even more thrilled to get to ride one of their horses.

Although the wind was whistling around them, Aislin found it surprisingly easy to hold a conversation. "I told your grandfather what my great-uncle said about the weapons Aghamonda plans to use," Tomas told her. "Your grandfather thinks it sounds as if Aghamonda has found some of the old magic. He didn't look at all happy."

"I bet he didn't," Aislin replied. Aghamonda was

doing exactly what the fairy king and queen had tried so hard to prevent. Unhappy was an understatement; her grandfather was probably furious.

They sped over farmland, through forests, and along a riverbank until they reached an area where the river ran wide and shallow through a sandy bed. Armies faced each other across the river where Aghamonda was already using her magic. As Aislin's party rode up, the fairy was waving her arms over the water, raising a mist that was so thick it was impossible to see through.

"Masks!" the fairy told the Scarmander troops, and they all slipped on small masks that covered their mouths and noses. When she pointed at the far side, the Duke of Isely led his troops across.

"I've seen enough. It's time to stop this," said King Darinar, and urged his horse toward Aghamonda.

"Stay here," King Carrigan told Aislin before following his father.

Poppy slipped off her horse's back, her legs shaking beneath her. She groaned in relief and led the horse to a nearby copse of trees while Aislin and Tomas watched what was happening on the river. As the Scarmander army reached the mist, the soldiers in front walked through it with their weapons raised as if there was nothing there. "The Morain army can't see them coming," Tomas said, urging his horse closer to Aislin's.

King Darinar and King Carrigan rode toward the mist ahead of the fairy warriors. The royals were almost upon it when the fairy king raised his arm and a light breeze dispersed the mist. On the other side, some soldiers fought with swords while others carried heavy sacks that they set in a pile just beyond the water's edge. A few soldiers were taking clay jars out of the sacks, opening them as they walked toward the men from Morain. Aislin recognized the sleeping mist that poured from the jars, and could sympathize with the soldiers who fell to the ground, unconscious. Suddenly the masks the Scarmander soldiers wore made sense.

Aislin stood in her stirrups, trying to get a better view. She spotted the Duke of Isely and King Tyburr hacking at each other with swords. Craiger was there too, fighting with two Scarmander soldiers at once. Most of the fiercest fighting was concentrated around them, although there were pockets of other fighters farther out.

When Aislin looked around, she saw Aghamonda

raise her arms and begin to turn in a circle. Water droplets rose from the river, collecting on the shore into large, blobby shapes. As the fairy turned faster, the shapes gained definition until the outlines of large cats appeared. In a moment, snarling, slinking felines were padding across the sand to attack soldiers from Morain with sharp teeth and claws. The soldiers fought back, hacking at the cats with their swords but slicing through with no effect.

"We have to help them!" Aislin cried, and urged her horse into the river. Tomas's horse plunged in after hers and they reached the other side together.

Aislin was passing the sacks that the Scarmander soldiers had left on the shoreline when she saw movement among the pile. The manticore and griffin were there, digging through them. She was about to ask what they were doing when one of the large cats pounced on a soldier only feet away. Sliding off her horse so that her feet were touching the ground, Aislin pulled power into herself and began to sing. The song was a simple one of earth, stone, and sand. It was enough to call the sand from the ground to whirl in the air in front of her. Mimicking Aghamonda, she created even bigger cats made of sand, with sharper teeth and longer claws. With her song propelling them, her cats sprang onto Aghamonda's creations, dragging them to the ground where they turned into puddles that disappeared into the sand, leaving the soldiers of Morain looking confused. When all of Aghamonda's cats had melted into the ground, Aislin ended her song.

Suddenly the sand-covered ground was gone from beneath their feet. In its place, a flat sheet of crystal extended as far as Aislin could see. Even the river she had just crossed was gone, leaving a slick surface that reflected the combatants and the sky above them. Soldiers who had been lunging at their opponents fell flat on their faces. Others slipped and slid as they tried to keep their footing. Once they fell, the crystal was so smooth that they could do little more than lie there. Only those who didn't try to move were still standing.

Aislin was almost convinced that the crystal was real until she sensed that the sand was still there; she just couldn't see it. The glamour was so realistic that only a fairy with great power could have created it. Having met Aghamonda, Aislin knew that she didn't have nearly enough power for such a glamour. It had to be either the king of the fairies or her own father. When she turned to look for them, she saw that King Darinar had called up the wind and was using it to propel

Aghamonda toward him. Even as she was swept across the crystal, the fairy woman flailed her arms, trying to use her own magic, but she was powerless against the fairy kings. The moment she reached them, the glamour vanished. Soldiers scrambled to their feet and the fighting began anew.

Aislin looked around to see what she could do to help stop the fighting. She saw Tomas battling alongside fairy warriors who were disarming the humans. When she spotted soldiers from Morain running toward them, she started singing again. This time she pulled boulders from deep within the ground to form walls, separating one group of soldiers from the other. The men fell back as the boulders piled themselves one on top of another.

The next time Aislin looked around, the fighting was nearly over. The fairy warriors were separating the soldiers and both the Duke of Isely and King Tyburr had laid down their arms. Leading her horse, Aislin returned to the shoreline where the manticore and the griffin were still digging through the sacks. "What are you doing?" she asked them.

"We're looking for Baibre. She's here somewhere. We can sense it," blared the manticore.

The griffin squawked and snagged a sack from the

268

bottom of the pile. Pulling it to the top, he ripped it open. There was only one thing inside.

"Twinket!" Aislin cried, reaching for her doll. To her horror, the doll was limp and looked lifeless in her hands.

Hearing Aislin's voice, Twinket opened one eye a crack. "Can I talk now?" she whispered.

"Yes," Aislin told her. "You're among friends."

With a squeal of delight, Twinket threw herself at Aislin and hugged her. "I thought I'd never see you again!"

Aislin hugged her back as hard as she could, saying, "I was afraid of that, too. I don't understand why Aghamonda took you."

"That was my fault," said Twinket. "She came looking for the locket. I'd hidden it in the best place I could think of—inside a tear that the trolls made in my side. She sensed where it was and took me, saying that I was as good a place to keep it as any. I guess I should have hidden it someplace better."

"It was a very good choice," the fairy king said, setting his hand on Aislin's shoulder. "May I see this locket?"

Aislin glanced toward Aghamonda, who was wrapped in vines and had a wad of leaves in her mouth.

"She is secured for now, but that's only temporary," said the fairy king. "I need to use something that will last long enough to transport her back to Fairengar for sentencing."

Aghamonda must have heard him, because her face turned pale and she began to squirm.

"What will happen to her?" Aislin asked.

"Whatever Queen Surinen and I decide after much deliberation," said her grandfather. "Throw her in a bottomless pit, take away her fairy powers, turn her into stone, feed her to the gargoyles…"

Aghamonda let out a muffled scream and struggled so much that she fell over and landed on her side. She began to roll until King Carrigan walked up and set his foot on her back, pinning her in place.

Twinket reached into the tear and pulled out the locket. "Here," she said, handing it to the fairy king. "I'm happy to get rid of it."

"I thought Poppy fixed all the holes," said Aislin.

Twinket shrugged. "She missed one, but she did such a good job with the others that I didn't want to complain."

King Darinar examined the locket and nodded. Walking back to where Aghamonda lay on the ground, he dangled the chain over her and motioned with his hand. With a bright light and a loud bang, the fairy was sucked into the locket with her sister.

"It's not very elegant," said the fairy king. "But it will do."

"Aren't you going to let Baibre out?" asked Aislin.

"I will when it's time for her to testify against her sister," King Darinar replied. "I think they have a lot to discuss and I'm giving them the time to do it."

"But Aghamonda still has those leaves in her mouth," Aislin reminded him.

"Yes, I know," said the fairy king. "It will be a very one-sided conversation. Aislin, I'd like to entrust you with taking the locket to your grandmother. I'd take it myself, but I'm going to stay here until I've seen that everything is worked out between Morain and Scarmander in an amicable manner. No fairy should have ever gotten involved in a human disagreement and I'm sorry it went as far as it did, but because a fairy was involved, I need to see it through to the end. Your father will take you home. Welcome back, sweet girl. We all missed you and worried about you constantly. You don't know how happy we are to have you back with us again. And I must tell you how proud I am of you. You were very brave and your talents have exceeded everyone's expectations. I didn't know that anyone could do what you did today. Who knows what you'll be able to do next!"

King Darinar's hug was enough to make Aislin squeak again. When the king walked off to speak to the Duke of Isely and King Tyburr, Aislin turned to Tomas. "I want to thank you for being nice to me when so many people were being unkind," she said. "You were my friend when I really needed one, and I want you to know that I'll be your friend forever."

Tomas grinned. "I liked you from the start. It was great to meet a good and decent person in that castle. If you ever need anything, just let me know. Although, with an army of fairies . . . I don't know what I could do that they couldn't."

"Friends are always important," Aislin told him. "And everyone has different talents."

"When will I see you again?" asked Tomas.

"Soon, I hope," Aislin said, and gave him a quick kiss on his cheek. "Right now I'm not sure what will happen next."

When Aislin turned away, half the troop of fairy warriors was waiting with her father and Poppy to take her home. Her heart swelled with pride when she saw them sitting astride their horses. She told herself that her eyes were watering because the light reflecting off their armor was so bright, but part of her knew that her tears were really those of joy at the thought of going home again.

Chapter 21

EVERY TIME AISLIN SAW Fairengar, she thought it had to have grown more beautiful than the last time she was there. Built of gold-veined marble, perfect crystals, moonbeams from clear nights, and sunbeams from cloudless days, it was the most beautiful building in the world. And she wasn't alone. Before Fairengar had been moved in entirety, people had traveled across countless kingdoms to see the fairy palace. Aislin had always thought it was a shame that more people didn't get to see it now. Returning home from the human lands, she wondered if that was about to change.

As beautiful as Fairengar was, Aislin thought the next sight she saw was even lovelier. Her mother waited just inside the palace gates, her face alight and her arms open to her daughter. With a cry from her heart, Aislin slipped from her horse and ran to her mother. Queen Maylin enfolded her in a warm embrace, murmuring soothing words just as she had when Aislin was a baby. When she finally held her daughter away from her to look her in the eyes, the pedrasi woman's smile faltered for an instant. "You've changed," she said. "You look older now. Did someone hurt you?"

"Not in any way that being home won't fix," Aislin told her mother, and gave her another hug.

Her mother smiled as King Carrigan took his daughter's hand and led them both inside. "I'm sure your grandmother is waiting for you in the throne room," he told Aislin. "She was ready to fly over the mountains and search all the human kingdoms for you herself. She'll want to welcome you back where everyone can see that you've returned, but we'll have a family celebration later when your grandfather is here."

"I'm very fortunate to have such a wonderful family," said Aislin.

"We're the ones who are fortunate," her father said. "You saved your mother and brother by sacrificing yourself. That was far more than anyone could ask or most would do."

Aislin shrugged. "My family is everything to

me. I would do anything and go anywhere to keep them safe."

"I believe that you and I have a lot to discuss," her father said.

"I have a lot to discuss with all of you," said Aislin.

The throne room was crowded when Aislin and her parents walked in. Fairies, sprites, nymphs, ogres, and other beings she had known all her life had come to welcome her back. The floor was marble, but the walls and ceiling were clear crystal so that it looked as if everyone was outside. Unlike those in the human kingdoms, the smiles that greeted her were genuine.

Although the thrones rested on a raised dais so that everyone could see the king and queen, neither the thrones nor the dais were at all like those in the human-owned castles. The thrones were made of the arched and curled branches of living trees, while the dais was made of rock taken straight from a glade in the woods. Moss and wildflowers spread across the rock's surface and small animals made their homes in the nooks and crannies. Water trickled down one side, magically replenishing itself as it gathered in a pool at the base. Occasionally, a frog croaked or a cricket chirped.

Although there weren't any trees in the room, the air was filled with the scents of the forest. Sometimes a bird flew through, but no one could see where they came from or where they went. When Aislin closed her eyes, it was easy to believe that she was in the forest itself.

This is what a throne room should be like, Aislin thought as she approached the throne.

Queen Surinen was smiling as her granddaughter drew closer. Aislin thought she was the most beautiful woman in the world, with hair the color of the moonless night sky and eyes the color of violets in the spring. Although the queen frowned as readily as she laughed, and she was older than most of her people could remember, her face was unlined and unblemished and had a radiance of its own.

"Welcome home," the queen told Aislin. "How are you after your grand adventure?"

Aislin grinned. "I'm well, Your Majesty." Their more informal greetings and their real conversation would come later when they didn't have an audience. Taking the locket from around her neck, she handed it to the sprite dressed all in green who waited at the foot of the dais. "King Darinar asked me to bring that to you," Aislin told her grandmother. "Two fairies are in there, but only one is waiting for sentencing."

The sprite darted up the dais, bowing his head when he handed the locket to the queen.

"Two?" the queen said as she examined the locket. "Oh, dear!"

"I have a lot to tell you," said Aislin.

The queen nodded. "And I have many questions for you."

The look they shared said a great deal. Things were going to change; they both knew it. Part of Aislin was sad because nothing was ever going to be the same again. But another part was excited—hiding from the humans hadn't worked, and now all the humans would know that the fairy king had come back. Perhaps it was time they returned to the world they'd left behind. Perhaps it was time the fairies helped to straighten up the mess that the human world had become. And perhaps it was time Aislin accepted herself for who she really was—a princess with powers that were unlike anyone else's.